*To my girlies with imposter syndrome:
you're already the main character,
but if you need to fake it until you make it...
I promise, no one can tell the difference.*

Behind the Scenes

The Backlot Series - Book 4

Kimberly Page

author's note

Dear Reader,

Welcome (back) to the fictional world of Hollywood! Stella and Brandon's story is a friends-to-lovers romance with one of my favorite tropes of all time: fake dating. There are no heavy trigger warnings here—unless you count mothers with strong opinions, society's outdated expectations, and a heroine who's spent way too much energy trying to be the "perfect" version of herself.

What I love about this book is how it explores that feeling so many of us know all too well: imposter syndrome. Stella thinks she has to perform her way into being enough, while Brandon has to figure out what his life looks like when the job he loves isn't as sustainable as it once was. Between the staged kisses and carefully crafted appearances, they discover that the most authentic thing of all might just be each other.

And of course—because this is a Backlot Series romance —there's plenty of humor, Hollywood drama, and open-door spice (consider this your NC-17 warning). Fake dating can only stay fake for so long before the sparks start flying.

I hope you love watching Stella and Brandon finally step into the spotlight they deserve.

Happy Reading!

💜 Kimberly

Crush - Tessa Violet
Too Sweet - Hozier
Close To You - Gracie Abrams
Style - Taylor Swift
Somebody To You - The Vamps
Nonsense - Sabrina Carpenter
Electric Love - BORNS
Bad Ideas - Tessa Violet
Sleeping With A Friend - Neon Trees
Everything Has Changed - Taylor Swift, Ed Sheeran
Dress - Taylor Swift
She Looks So Perfect - 5 Seconds of Summer
If You Love Her - Forest Blakk
Tongue Tied - GROUPLOVE
we can't be friends (wait for your love) - Ariana Grande
Ruin The Friendship - Taylor Swift
The Only Exception - Paramore
back to friends - sombr
Lucky - Jason Mraz, Colbie Caillat
This Feeling - The Chainsmokers, Kelsea Ballerini
Everywhere, Everything - Noah Kahan

one

. . .

Stella

POWER ON A HOLLYWOOD studio lot looks a lot like riding around in a golf cart, and today, Blair lets me drive.

The electric hum kicks under my palms, quiet and smug, as we zip past a row of grip trucks and a family of tourists who strain to see if we're anyone famous. The air smells like fresh paint, hot concrete, and a hint of sweetness coming from the orange trees planted around the edges of the studio's backlot. Sunlight slices across the façades. New York street to our left, Midwest town square to our right. A sky that is forever California blue above it all.

Blair Bennett, my boss and mentor, sits beside me in oversized sunglasses, her hand resting casually on the curve of her very obvious baby bump. Even nine months pregnant, she manages to look like the sharpest person on the lot in a tailored black dress, heels I wouldn't dare attempt, and her one allotted coffee of the day balanced within easy reach. Blair isn't just my boss; she's *the* Blair Bennett, a former power player at The Wynn Agency and now the founder of

Tangerine Talent and one of the most respected agents in Hollywood. She's the woman who plucked me out of USC for an internship and showed me what ambition actually looks like.

We glide to a stop outside the bungalow where Ava St. James holds court. One of those orange trees is artfully planted in a barrel that guards the door, and a PA checks our names like he's protecting state secrets before waving us in. Ava is an icon, the kind who rose to fame in the mid-2000s, claimed an Oscar and a shelf of other awards, and built her reputation on being part of Hollywood's elite. But the industry is shifting with every year, and so are the opportunities. If we're lucky, today might be the day she finally agrees to expand her definition of what success looks like.

Inside, the air is cool, the walls lined with framed black-and-whites of the actors and actresses who built this studio.

"Ladies." Ava rises from the couch, elegance wrapped in linen and an easy smile. Her eyes drop to Blair's stomach and soften. "Look at you. Glowing. And I say that as someone who loathes that phrase."

Blair opens her arms. "Trying to make it my brand."

They hug, and I hang back, trying not to interrupt the moment. This is Blair's final meeting before her scheduled C-section on Monday. Yes, Monday, because that woman is only giving herself a weekend break before she goes on maternity leave. Which means, for the next few months, it'll be me stepping into her shoes.

We sit, and Blair dives right in, giving Ava the news we came to share. "Two offers this week. One's a therapist role, the older-but-wise woman who pushes the protagonist toward her breakthrough. The other is a grandmother in a studio comedy."

Ava tips her head, her irritation sharp. "I didn't claw my way to an Oscar to be cast in a sitcom as some elderly babysitter."

Blair leans forward, calm and unbothered. "They're circling you for gravitas. But it's your call. What's your instinct?"

Ava hesitates, then glances at me. "What do *you* think, Stella? Fresh eyes."

Heat prickles my collar. I'm just here to observe. But Blair gives me the smallest nod, that silent permission slip that says I'm okay to share my thoughts.

"I think..." I start carefully, weighing each word. "The therapist role has more depth than the grandmother. But I also think your audience would grow if you considered options outside traditional films. Streaming series, prestige TV...it's where some of the most layered roles are happening right now."

Ava studies me, her lips quirking, not offended but not converted, either. "So, you're telling me to trade the silver screen for someone's laptop."

"Not trade," I say quickly. "Expand."

She smiles kindly, though it doesn't reach her eyes. "You're sharp. I like that. But I'm still a movie actress."

Blair lets the moment settle. "Then let's say yes to the therapist and pass on the grandmother. Stella will keep things moving while I'm out. You'll be in excellent hands."

Ava turns to me again, her hands cool and elegant around mine. "Well, Stella, it shouldn't be too hard to manage a client whose career's circling the drain." The smile she adds makes it sound like a joke, though there's steel underneath.

My throat tightens, but I hold her gaze. "I wouldn't call it that. I think people are still lining up to work with you—and they should be."

Ava's laugh lingers as she turns away, already signaling to her assistant that we're done here. The meeting ends with polite goodbyes, though the weight of her words presses against my chest long after we step into the sun.

It's not that Ava's wrong. In Hollywood, a man in his forties is just hitting his stride, offered leading roles against women twenty years younger. A woman the same age? She's fighting for scraps, not because she's any less talented, but because the system decides she's less sellable. The stories we tell still belong to men.

Blair slips on her sunglasses as we step into the sunlight. "I didn't spell it out for Ava, but here's the deal—she's yours while I'm out. Think of it as a trial run. If you keep things steady, she'll stay with you permanently."

My pulse jumps. "Wait, seriously?"

Blair takes a measured sip of coffee. "You've been ready for this. All you have to do now is not fuck it up."

Words tangle in my throat, and she cuts me off with a look. "Don't overthink it, Stella. Just do what you do best. You'll nail this."

Blair checks her phone, then tucks it away. "I'm heading over to Building A to see Wyatt and steal him for lunch before my next meeting. Can you get the cart back to the return and make it to the office on your own?"

I nod, watching her gather her things. It still feels surreal sometimes, seeing Blair with Wyatt—her high school boyfriend, whom she reconnected with a few years ago through work. I'd witnessed their awkward reunion firsthand, watching Blair try to stay professional while clearly being affected by seeing him again. Now they're married and expecting their first child together.

"Of course," I say quickly. My pulse is still thudding, but I manage a smile. "Actually, I was going to swing by and see Brandon while I'm here. He's shooting on New York Street today."

Blair's mouth quirks. "Tell him to try not to break his neck before the weekend."

"I will, and give Wyatt my best."

She gives my arm a squeeze, then heads off, already dialing Wyatt, leaving me with the cart, the sun, and the kind of news I can't wait to tell Brandon first.

Brandon Grimaldi is a professional stuntman, one of the guys you've likely seen fly through a window or get set on fire in a blockbuster, even if you didn't know it was him. Around here, he's the one directors trust to step in when it gets a little too real for the star of the show.

He also happens to be my across-the-hall neighbor and the honorary guy at our girls' nights. Perpetually single but never short on dates, he's easygoing and fun, the kind of guy who makes every room feel lighter. Somehow, he and I have landed on a weekly tradition—takeout and reality TV, with both of us taking turns with color commentary.

Ava meeting done. I have news. Where are
you on the lot?

New York Street. North end. Big fake deli.
They have real pickles, though. Come
steal one.

I bite back a smile I feel all the way down to my toes. Of all the things Los Angeles has given me, Brandon ranks unreasonably high. He's older, steady in a way that makes me feel both safe and a little reckless. Strong in all the obvious ways, the kind of man who looks like he was born knowing how to lift people out of burning buildings. And unfairly hot—so much so that if we hadn't met as neighbors and friends first, I probably never would've had the nerve to talk to him. Women notice him everywhere, and for a while, it felt like there was a new face on his arm every other week. Lately, though...I can't actually remember the last time I saw him with anyone.

The second I press the pedal, the cart gives its usual dramatic bucking launch before settling into a hum. I weave through the lot, past extras sweating in fake wool coats, past a fountain that, tomorrow, will either host a love confession or a body dump. New York Street appears like a magic trick, its façades stacked side by side, not a real home in sight. And there, just like he promised, is the fake deli with the pastrami special no one will ever order.

Brandon leans against the craft services table, a pickle in hand, breaking every heart within a fifty-foot radius. His T-shirt stretches over his biceps like the fabric's barely keeping up, and his hair—too long, always falling into his eyes—gets pushed back with a casual sweep of his hand. When his gaze lifts and lands on me, I swear it sharpens, brightens, like I'm the one he was waiting for. Then comes that easy, devastating smile with perfectly straight white teeth. He is the poster child for heartbreaker.

He walks over to me, smelling like sunshine and fake deli. "There she is!"

"You promised pickles."

"That, I did." He plucks a cup off the craft services table, dropping one inside before handing it over like it's contraband. "Look at that. Dreams really do come true."

I bite into it, and the crunch echoes in my ears. "Okay, that's better than I expected."

Brandon grins. "Right?"

I smile around another bite. "How was your morning?"

"Nope, we're not talking about me." His gaze sharpens, teasing but curious. "Spill."

I shift the cup in my hands as energy buzzes in my chest. "Blair wants me to manage Ava St. James while she's out on maternity leave. If I do well..." My throat catches. "She could stay my client."

Brandon doesn't even blink. His grin breaks wide, warm and proud, like he's been expecting this all along. He takes my elbows, steadying me. "Of course she did. Stell, you're gonna crush it. I never doubted it for a second."

The knot in my chest eases. "You really think so?"

"I know so."

He gives my arms a quick squeeze, but before I can reply,

a set assistant jogs up, her headset slipping down her cheek. "Brandon, they're ready for you on mark."

He groans good-naturedly, already backing toward the street. "Duty calls. Can you stick around for a bit? Watch me work?"

"Just one scene," I say, trying to sound firm even as my chest warms at the invitation.

For a breath, it feels almost like I've got everything I've ever wanted.

two

. . .

Brandon

THE EXPLOSION RATTLES MY TEETH, even through the safety gear, and I'm already moving before the debris settles. Twenty-foot fall, backwards, into what looks like a pile of rubble but is meticulously placed padding designed to look like concrete chunks. I've done this exact stunt probably fifty times in my career, but today, something feels different.

I hit the landing and roll, just like I'm supposed to. The crowd of crew members erupts in applause, and I flash them the trademark grin that's gotten me through fourteen years in this business. But when I push myself up from the mats, there's a half-second hesitation that wasn't there a few years ago. My left shoulder protests just enough to remind me it's been dislocated twice in the past three years.

"Beautiful work, Grimaldi!" Tony Ricci, the stunt coordinator, jogs over with a relieved smile. "That's a wrap."

I dust off the fake concrete powder and accept the towel someone hands me. "Thanks, man. The timing felt good."

It did feel good. That's not the problem. The problem is the tiny voice in the back of my head that's started asking questions I don't want to answer. Questions like how many more falls I've got left in me and what the hell I'm going to do when the answer is zero. At thirty-two years old, I'm painfully aware that I don't have a whole lot of time left in the stunt-double game. Many retire by forty due to an accumulation of injuries.

"Brandon!" Jade Martinez, the film's lead actress, bounces over in her post-explosion makeup. Though covered in soot streaks and fake blood, she's grinning like a kid at Christmas. "That was insane. I can't believe you just threw yourself off a building for me."

"All in a day's work," I tell her as we head over to the craft services area. "Besides, I love getting to make you look like the badass you are."

This is one of my favorite parts of the job, honestly. More and more films are featuring women in action roles, and I'm here for all of it. Growing up with six sisters taught me that women are plenty tough on their own, and if all they need is someone to help sell it on screen, I'm happy to do it. Jade is playing a former Army medic turned vigilante, and watching her own her character's physicality has been the highlight of this shoot.

"Seriously, though," she says, "I don't know how you do it. Aren't you scared?" The honest answer is it's trust I worry about. Everything in this job comes down to it—trusting the riggers, the spotters, the crew. Fear only creeps in when the trust isn't there. Same goes for real life. Trust is everything.

But Jade doesn't need to hear that. "Nah. I've got the best safety team in the business looking out for me."

It's true. Tony runs the tightest operation in Hollywood, and I trust him with my life on a daily basis. The fact that my body is starting to feel every single one of those calculated risks is my problem, not his.

"You've got thirty minutes," Tony calls out. "Then we're moving to the car sequence."

I continue to the craft services table, nodding at familiar faces along the way. This is a good crew, people I've worked with on at least a dozen other films. There's something comforting about the routine of it all. Show up, do something that should probably kill you, go home in one piece. Repeat.

I'm reaching for a bottle of water when I spot her.

Stella threads her way across the sound stage like she owns it, her heels steady against the concrete as she sidesteps cables and crew with practiced ease. She's all business in that tailored blazer, her blonde hair pulled back sharply, her phone already out like she's mentally three steps ahead of whatever meeting she just left.

A grip does a double-take as she passes, nearly dropping the light stand he's carrying. His buddy elbows him and says something I can't hear, and they both watch her walk by. She doesn't even notice, too focused on whatever email she's typing.

Typical.

Two PAs by the stunt setup stop mid-conversation when she asks where to find me, and they stumble over themselves to point toward the craft services table. She thanks them with that warm smile of hers and keeps moving, completely missing the way they track her across the room.

I grit my teeth, biting back a laugh.

She's Blair Bennett's right hand, a rising star at Tangerine Talent, the kind of agent who can negotiate a deal that leaves everyone feeling like they won. In a professional setting, she's unstoppable. Confident, sharp, always three moves ahead. But the second it shifts to anything personal, anything that even hints at someone being interested in her? She's completely oblivious.

"Hey, sunshine," I call when she's close enough. "Any notes?"

She spots me, and that smile hits me square in the chest—bright, easy, like I'm her favorite part of the day.

The truth is, Stella's gorgeous. Always has been. If she hadn't been immediately classified as friend territory when we met, I probably would've tried to hit on her. Turned out better this way, and I wouldn't want to mess up what we have for anything.

She's petite enough that I could scoop her up without breaking a sweat, but she carries herself like she's six feet tall when she's negotiating a contract. She's got that natural pretty combined with Southern charm she doesn't even know she's wielding. What kills me is she has no idea of the effect she has on people, especially men. She's so focused on the work, on taking care of everyone else, that she completely misses when someone's interested.

Case in point: that grip is still staring, and she hasn't noticed once.

"That was incredible," she says, her voice threaded with awe. "I don't know how you do it."

I grin and take a swig from the bottle to keep my answer in check. "Just another day at the office."

I give her the quick tour of my latest set, pointing out the safety rigs and explaining how we make it look like I'm actually falling to my death instead of landing on a pile of very expensive padding. Stella asks smart questions, the kind that prove she's picked up more about the technical side of production for films in her few years in the business than most people learn in a decade. She's got good instincts, and it shows in how quickly she's risen at Tangerine Talent.

"It's amazing," she says when I finish. "I mean, I knew it was complicated, but seeing it up close..." She shakes her head. "No wonder actors love working with you."

"Just part of the job." I grab another water and offer her one. "You want to stick around and watch me crash a car?"

"I wish I could, but I've got another meeting back at the office in half an hour." She checks her phone and winces. "I should probably go."

"Come on," I say, nodding toward the cart she left parked nearby. "I'll drive you over, and then I'll bring this back so you don't have to worry about it."

Her shoulders drop with relief. "You're a lifesaver. These shoes weren't built for cross-lot treks."

When I pull up to the garage, she hops out and leans on the edge of the cart for a beat.

"Thanks again. I had a blast watching you today."

"Thanks for sticking around. And sunshine? Congrats

again. You've worked your ass off, and you've earned every bit of this opportunity. I'm proud of you."

Her grin softens, and for a second I swear she's about to say something else. Instead, she just nods.

"We're still on for tonight?" I ask. "I'll grab food."

"Yep, sounds good. See you tonight!"

She waves once more before heading inside, and I sit there a moment longer than I should, watching her disappear, before turning the cart back toward the lot. Stella's one of the good ones, the kind of friend who makes everything better just by showing up.

When I return to the soundstage, Tony appears with my helmet and the kind of grin that means I'm about to do something spectacular. "Time to make this car fly."

Right now, I've got a job to do, and despite the growing voice of doubt in my head, I'm still pretty damn good at it.

The car sequence goes perfectly. I crash through two fake walls and flip the vehicle exactly where it's supposed to land, rolling out with the kind of precision that only comes from years of practice. The crew cheers, Tony looks relieved, and I feel that familiar rush of satisfaction that comes from nailing a difficult stunt.

But when I'm changing out of my safety gear twenty minutes later, my shoulder protests just enough to remind me that perfect execution might not be enough to keep me in the game forever.

three

. . .

Stella

I HEAR the unmistakable sound of Brandon's boots echoing on the pavement just as I'm pulling my bag from the backseat of my car.

"You stalking me, Rhodes?" he calls across the garage.

I roll my eyes as we fall into step, both heading toward the elevator. "Yes, Brandon. My entire schedule revolves around the hope that I'll catch you in your post-work glory, carrying..." I take a whiff of the bag he's holding and catch the delicious garlic scent. "Italian food, like a knight with a plastic fork."

He holds up the bag. "Extra garlic knots, as requested. And I talked them into extra marinara. We're living large tonight."

"It smells incredible," I groan.

The elevator dings, and we step inside. It's just the two of us, and I shift my bag higher on my shoulder as he hits the button for our floor.

"You hear about Jess's interview with that actress from *Spiraling*?" he asks, leaning casually against the wall.

Jess Lexington is a sharp-tongued entertainment reporter who built her career exposing powerful men in Hollywood. She and Brandon have been close friends for years—which is actually how I met him in the first place. She accidentally married Lucas Carmichael, a studio PR man who used to be her favorite on-record target. They were rivals until they weren't, and when their fake marriage turned into something real, she gave up her apartment across from Brandon to move in with Lucas. I inherited her lease and her neighbor, which turned out to be the deal of a lifetime.

"Did I?" I grin. "That clip's been everywhere. Blair said the studio's doing damage control because of what the actress said about the director."

"I mean…Jess *did* bait her."

"That's her job," I say, amused. "She always asks the questions people want answers to."

He nods. "You think she gets death threats?"

"Oh, definitely. Probably framed the first one."

We both laugh, and it's just easy. This is what I love about Brandon: he lets me be me. No pressure. No pretending. Just this rhythm we've fallen into, like we've known each other forever.

The elevator dings as it reaches the first-floor lobby, and the doors slide open. Then I see him.

Mason Park.

The devastatingly handsome neighbor I've been quietly obsessing over for months while simultaneously avoiding any meaningful conversation because, apparently, proximity to him turns me into a socially incompetent disaster. My stomach drops like I'm on a roller coaster that just hit the steepest part of the track.

He's standing there in joggers and a fitted tee that clings in all the right places, and I can't stop myself from cataloging every perfect detail. Perfectly tousled blonde hair. Bright blue eyes that crinkle slightly at the corners. A jawline sharp enough to cut glass. You know, the kind of classic good looks that belong in old Hollywood movies. His tan skin has that effortless California glow, and the way his shirt fits across his chest and shoulders makes my mouth go dry.

Well, this is just fantastic.

I paste on my best pageant smile, the kind I perfected at sixteen back home in Georgia for cotillions and fundraising galas. Bright. Polite. Quiet.

"Hey, Stella," he says like it's normal. "Hey, Brandon."

Brandon gives him the kind of nod only guys understand. "What's up, man?"

I remain silent because, apparently, twenty-five years of being told that men prefer women who are agreeable and soft-spoken has left me completely incapable of normal conversation with attractive guys. It's maddening. I can go toe-to-toe with studio executives and come out winning, but put me in an elevator with a cute guy, and suddenly, I'm back to practicing the art of being seen and not heard.

The elevator dings again as we reach our floor. Mason glances up, pockets his phone, and flashes me that smile that turns my brain to mush.

"You two have a good night," he says as he exits through the open doors.

"You, too," Brandon replies.

I make a sound that might be words, might be a sneeze, and then race in the opposite direction to my apartment before I finally let myself breathe.

Brandon follows me to my door and, with one brow raised, asks, "What. Was. That."

"I panicked."

"Was that a stroke? Should I call someone?"

"Shut up," I mutter, fumbling my keys so badly I nearly drop them. He plucks them out of the air before they hit the ground and hands them back with maddening calm.

"I've never seen you malfunction like that. You froze so hard I almost threw a coat over you and declared it winter."

"I have a crush, okay? A stupid, completely impractical, Mason-shaped crush."

"Yeah, I picked up on that." Brandon's grin is entirely too amused. "The statue impression was a dead giveaway."

"It's not funny!"

"It's a little funny. You literally didn't say a single word the entire time."

I slump against my doorframe. "It's pathetic."

"So, why don't you just talk to him next time?"

"Because I'll probably say something mortifying and ruin any chance I might have had."

"Chance at what? You want him to ask you out?"

"I mean...yeah. That would be nice. But it's probably better that he hasn't since I can't even string together a coherent sentence when he's around."

"Well, you're in luck," Brandon says, stepping inside like

he owns the place. "Because these garlic knots don't care how weird you are."

By the time I shut the door behind us, I'm still embarrassed, but then the smell of the food hits me, and just like that, my favorite Thursday tradition brings me to a happy place.

"You wanna change?" he asks over his shoulder as he starts setting the takeout on the coffee table. "I'll set it up."

"I do. And I don't say this lightly... Thank you for rescuing me from both cooking and pants."

"You're welcome. But please do put on some kind of pants." His voice gets louder as I walk out of the room and down the hall. "You can pay me back with one of your home-made desserts."

"Done!" I'm grinning as I disappear into the bedroom. I swap my pencil skirt and blazer for soft shorts and a tank, twist my hair into a bun, and return to find Brandon's spread of plates, napkins, and utensils and arranged food. He's sitting on his side of the sectional, already halfway through his garlic bread.

"Yours is the chicken parm," he says, pointing with a fork. "I got us both the salad we like. And if you touch my cannoli without asking, I can't be held responsible for what might happen."

"Noted."

I slide onto the couch and pull my plate toward me. Without thinking, I reach over and steal some of his chicken marsala. He doesn't even blink. Two bites later, he's cutting off a piece of chicken parm from my plate.

"How do you do it?" I blurt out , then immediately regret

how desperate it sounds. "I mean...how are you so sure of yourself with people?"

Brandon laughs, but not in a mean way. "You think I'm sure of myself? Stella, half the time I'm just winging it and hoping nobody notices."

He takes another bite. "But here's the thing. Even when I'm nervous or don't know what I'm doing, I act like I do. Fake it till you make it actually works. Your brain starts to believe what you're telling it. Also, turns out most people are too worried about their own stuff to judge you as harshly as you think they are."

"I think my problem is I don't even know what confident looks like when it comes to dating. Like, what am I supposed to fake? Flirting? Being charming? I have no idea what I'm aiming for." I slump back against the couch.

"You aim to be yourself. Your thoughts, your wants, your presence—they all matter. And any man worth your time will want to see all of that, not some watered-down version you think he'll approve of."

I nod, but the swirl in my chest doesn't quiet. It's a mix of nerves and pressure and something else I don't know how to describe just yet.

Brandon stabs another piece of chicken off my plate without asking.

"If you wanted chicken parm, why didn't you get your own?"

He just smirks like he knows exactly what he's doing.

I shake my head and lean back, studying him for a beat. "You just make everything look easy."

"That's because it is easy," he says around another stolen bite.

"Not for me." I swirl my glass in my hand, and the thought slips out before I can stop it. "Maybe one day you'll have to teach me how you do it."

His grin tilts, lazy and amused. "Careful, Rhodes. You ask for lessons, I'm charging by the hour."

I laugh and clink my glass against his, brushing it off like a joke. But somewhere in the back of my mind, the idea of Brandon actually teaching me doesn't sound like the worst thing.

four

. . .

Stella

I'M BALANCING on one leg, with the other extended behind me, trying to focus on breathing through my nose while thinking about the off-handed comment Brandon made last night about lessons. I want them. The idea that he could help me get more comfortable and confident around guys makes my heart rate pick up, which isn't helping my already wobbly balance.

I lower my back leg and step into a deep lunge, feeling the stretch along my hip. Then I slowly rise, turning my back foot sideways and sinking into a wide stance. My heel presses down, steady and strong, as I extend my arms out to either side. I root through my feet and breathe into the stretch, letting my mind float back to the possibility of no longer being the single girl in a sea of couples. My mother would be ecstatic.

Natalie's voice floats through the room. "Ground through your feet. Find where you're holding tension. Let it go."

I take a deep breath and think about all the tension that

would be released if I could actually get a date and some regular sex. It's not exactly my mom's version of happily ever after, but to be fair, that looks more like me being married by now. She wants wedding bells and grandchildren. The fact that I'm twenty-five and single is basically a personal failing on my part—never mind that I have a career I love and a life that's actually pretty great.

It's not that my mother's pushing is mean-spirited—quite the opposite. She genuinely wants me to be happy, settled, and taken care of. The problem is, I'm just not sure that is my idea of happiness.

Class ends with a long savasana, and I let myself melt into the mat. Natalie dims the lights and moves through the room with effortless grace. And even though she's wearing a lavender crop top and speaks with a soothing, soft voice, she still radiates don't-mess-with-me energy.

When she dismisses us, I roll up my mat and make my way to the front desk to find my bestie.

Natalie Cruz is a fiercely loyal friend who'll hex your ex and then hand you a turmeric latte without breaking a sweat. Her dark hair is braided down her back, streaked with violet, and there's an intricate constellation map tattooed along her left forearm, delicate lines connecting tiny stars that seem to shimmer when she moves.

She's got that post-class glow and the kind of I-don't-care confidence that's completely earned.

Born and raised in LA, she knows every hidden trail, underground supper club, and parking trick in this city. We became inseparable after I wandered into this very class two years ago.

"Time for breakfast?" I ask her.

"Yes, I'm starving."

We walk to the café across the street, and Natalie orders a green tea and mango açaí bowl. I go for a breakfast sandwich and an extra-large vanilla latte. We claim a table on the sidewalk patio; the metal chairs are still cool from sitting in the morning's shadows.

Natalie settles into her chair with the fluid grace of someone who's spent years perfecting her posture, crossing one impossibly long leg over the other. She wraps her hands around her mug and, as steam curls up from it to catch the morning light, fixes me with those sharp green eyes that have a way of seeing straight through whatever mask you're wearing.

"What?"

"You seem stressed," she says.

I take a sip of my coffee. "I'm not stressed. Just thinking."

"Want to talk about it?"

I pause, peeling back the wrapper on my sandwich. "Well, first, I found out I get to manage Ava St. James while Blair is out on maternity leave."

"Holy shit. That's amazing, Stella. Congrats!"

I can't help the smile that creeps across my lips as I take a bite. I'm still so excited about the assignment. "Thanks. If only my mom felt the same."

"I'm not following."

"Oh, I'm just bitching. My mom sent me a text this morning trying to set me up with the son of one of her friends who just moved out here. Apparently, he's very polite, very stable, and—her words, not mine—very ready to settle down."

Natalie raises one perfectly shaped brow. "How romantic."

"She included a photo. It's giving insurance brochure."

"Is he holding a Labrador and standing in front of a kayak?"

"Golden retriever. Canoe."

"Close enough."

We both laugh, and I already feel the tension melting. Natalie has a way of making me feel better about what's bothering me.

"I know she means well," I say. "But one minute, I'm on top of the world, feeling successful and proud of myself, and then I get a message from her, and it's hard not to feel like I'm failing some invisible checklist."

Natalie leans forward, resting her elbows on the table. "What do you mean by 'checklist'?"

I take a breath. "It's like I won't be successful in her eyes until I'm all wifed up."

Natalie almost spits out her tea. "Do you even want to date?"

"I mean, I'm not gonna say no to a date. It wouldn't be the worst to find a hot guy who wants to pamper me, buy me dinner, and give me good sex."

She snorts out a laugh. "Well, is there anyone you have your eyes on?"

I shrug.

She tilts her head. "What about Brandon?"

The question blindsides me. "What?"

"Brandon. You've said he's hot. And funny. And sweet. And I'm sure he could give you the good sex you're after."

"He's my friend."

Natalie raises one shoulder, unbothered. "So?"

"So, he's Brandon. We watch *Love Island* and eat sushi off paper towels. It's not like that."

She gives me a look. "I'm just saying, if he looked at me the way he looks at you, I'd have climbed him like a tree ages ago."

My stomach flips. I brush it off. "It's not Brandon."

"Then who?"

I hesitate. There's a beat of silence. Then I take a sip of my coffee and say, "His name's Mason. He lives in my building."

Natalie sits back, her eyes lighting up with interest. "Ohhh. The hallway crush."

I nod miserably. "I keep running into him, and I keep embarrassing myself. I saw him in the elevator last week, and I couldn't even say hi. Just stood there like a deer in headlights."

"I'm sure it wasn't that bad."

"Brandon even asked me what the hell my problem was," I tell her as my head falls into my hands in dramatic fashion.

She shrugs. "So, ask him out."

I shake my head. "Natalie, you don't understand. This man is...he's Superman hot—David Corenswet version—and I turn into a mute statue every time I see him."

"Have you seen you?" she shoots back. "Stella, you're gorgeous, successful, funny when you're not overthinking yourself into paralysis. Any man would be lucky to have your attention."

"You're biased."

"Absolutely, I am, but that doesn't make me wrong. Here's a crazy idea—you could just knock on his door and ask if he wants to go grab coffee."

I nearly choke on my latte. "I couldn't. There's no way I have the nerve for that."

"Why not? What's the worst that could happen?"

"He could say no, and then I'd have to move out of the building in shame."

"Or he could say yes, and you could stop torturing yourself with elevator small talk, or in your case, no talk."

I'm quiet for a minute. "There is one thing I've been thinking about."

She waits for me to continue, and when I don't, she puts her hand out and motions for me to go on.

"Last night, I made a comment to Brandon that I wish I had his confidence."

"Yeah, we all do."

"He said something about giving me lessons."

She leans forward and rests her chin on her hand. "What kind of lessons?"

I shrug. "How to be confident, I guess?"

Natalie is just staring at me.

"What?"

"It's not the worst idea I've heard." She checks her phone and sighs. "I have to get back for my next class, but if it's a man you're looking for, then I say go after what you want."

"Yeah, maybe."

Natalie just smiles. "I'm just saying. You've gotten everything else you've wanted. Why not this?"

It's a good question.

"See you soon?"

"You know it, babe. Love ya!"

After she leaves, I sit there for a moment, turning her words over in my mind. Maybe she's right. Maybe I should stop overthinking and just go after what I want. The question is figuring out exactly what that looks like and working up the nerve to do it.

I check the time on my phone. Brandon's probably finished his Sunday morning family call by now. I can picture him in his kitchen, still in whatever he slept in, surviving on nothing but coffee because he had good intentions of making breakfast but got distracted by his sisters' latest drama or his mom asking when he's coming home for a visit.

Without really thinking about it, I get up and walk back to the counter, where the barista is cleaning espresso cups.

"Excuse me," I say. "Could I get an avocado bacon Benedict to go? And maybe throw in one of those almond croissants?"

It's his favorite weekend order. I try to bring him food from here when I take Nat's class. For now, it's Brandon I bring food to. Maybe, if I can figure out how to form actual words around attractive men, Mason could be next.

five

Brandon

THE MORNING SUN streams through my apartment windows as I balance my laptop on my knees, trying to look presentable for the family FaceTime call that's become a weekly routine. On my screen, the familiar faces around the Grimaldi family dining room come into view. My parents are at the head of the table, and my six sisters are scattered around with various husbands and children, creating the beautiful chaos of voices and laughter.

"Hey, Brandon!" My oldest sister, Nina, waves at the camera while simultaneously trying to keep her three-year-old from launching himself off his chair.

My mother appears, squinting like it will help her see me better through the small screen. "Are you getting enough to eat? You look thin."

"Yes, Ma, I'm eating enough," I dutifully report, which makes my mother, Maria Grimaldi, narrow her eyes at me through the screen.

"Show me your refrigerator," she demands in that tone that still makes me feel twelve years old, even at thirty-two.

"Ma, I'm not showing you my refrigerator."

She turns to my father, who's carving what looks like the most perfect roast beef in the history of roast beef. "Nick, your son is going to waste away to nothing in that Hollywood apartment."

My father, ever the diplomat, just chuckles and continues carving. After forty-five years of marriage and raising seven children, he's learned when to engage and when to let his wife's worry run its course.

The Grimaldi family story starts with my great-grandparents, who arrived from Sicily in the 1920s with nothing but determination and a dream of building something lasting. They started with the Grimaldi Grande, a single hotel in Manhattan that became the foundation of Grimaldi Hotels and Resorts, now one of the most respected luxury resort chains in the country.

Fast forward three generations later, and my parents, Maria and Nick Grimaldi, met in high school, fell in love, married, and had seven beautiful children, who were all expected to carry on the family legacy. Nina, Isabella, the twins, Valentina and Victoria, Ariana, Giuliana, and me, the baby of the family.

Everyone found their place in the business. Nina runs operations, Isabella handles marketing, the twins manage different properties, Ariana oversees guest relations, and Giuliana runs food services.

Then there's me, the one who looked at a life of luxury

hotels and five-star service and decided I'd rather throw myself off buildings for a living.

My parents have always been supportive, but I know there's a corner office with my name on it waiting for me whenever I'm ready to come home to the family business.

"I'm hardly wasting away," I protest, flexing my arm toward the camera. "Stunts keep me in pretty good shape."

"Oh, my God, Brandon!" Isabella suddenly sits up straighter, nearly knocking over a glass. "Marco and I finally watched that action movie you were in. I swear I could tell which stunts were actually you and which were the other guys."

"Really?" I can't help but grin. My family doesn't always understand what I do, but they're genuinely proud when they see the finished product.

"The motorcycle chase through downtown," she continues excitedly. "That was you, wasn't it?"

"Guilty as charged."

"It looked incredible," Nina chimes in. "Terrifying but incredible. How's everything going with work? You seem busier than ever."

"It's good. Really good, actually. I'm booked solid through the summer." I pause, then add with a casualness I don't quite feel, "Though I'll be honest. This body won't last forever. I'm starting to think about what comes next."

The admission surprises me as much as it does them. I hadn't planned on being that vulnerable, but something about being around all of them right now makes me more honest than I usually am.

"That's smart," my father says, his voice carrying that

quiet wisdom that always made us kids feel heard rather than judged. "You've built something incredible, son. Whatever direction you want to take it, we're behind you.

"You know," he continues casually, raising a fork to eat, "We've been renovating the Malibu property. If you ever want to explore options that keep you close to the film industry but maybe a little easier on the joints, there's always room for you with Grimaldi Resorts. But only if that's something you want."

There's no pressure in his voice, just love and support wrapped in a practical offer.

"I appreciate that, Dad. Really."

The conversation naturally shifts to lighter topics, including Isabella's new house renovation and the ongoing planning of Giuliana's engagement party. But my father's words linger, not as pressure but as possibility.

"Exactly. Which means Brandon's officially the last hold-out." Nina grins wickedly at the camera.

I missed what they were talking about, but I can guess it likely started with my mother's desire for more grandchildren and the fact that Giuliana's the last of the sisters to get married.

"There's nothing wrong with being single," I say, trying to jump back into the conversation.

"Of course there isn't," my father says, his voice carrying that quiet authority. "But Brandon, son, there's also nothing wrong with wanting more than just work."

"We just want you happy, B," Valentina says. "Whatever that looks like."

"Speaking of happy," Isabella chimes in, and I can practically hear the mischief in her voice, "anyone special we should know about? It would be amazing if you finally brought someone home for us to meet."

I lean back against my couch, suddenly grateful for the three thousand miles between us. "Not really my priority right now."

"Come on," Giuliana presses. "You're in the land of beautiful people. Surely, there's someone interesting."

"Dating in LA is a lot like dating in Brooklyn as a Grimaldi," I say, the words coming out more cynical than I intended. "You're never really sure if someone's with you for your winning personality or because they've done the math on what the family name might mean for them."

The line goes quiet for a moment.

"Oh, honey." My mother's voice is soft with understanding. "Not everyone you meet will be that way."

"It's just easier to keep things casual," I add quickly, not wanting to bring down the mood. "Less complicated."

"Brandon," my father says gently, "the right person won't care about any of that. They'll just care about you."

"I know." I want to believe that's true, but I just don't have that experience yet. Back home in New York, it was my bank account people seemed to love. Here, the money is assumed, and it's more my connections and if I can help someone catch their big break, too.

After the goodbyes and the final waves, I close my laptop and sit in the sudden quiet of my apartment. The truth is, I am happy. I love what I do, love the adrenaline, technical challenge, and camaraderie of film sets. I love the freedom to take jobs that interest me, to travel, to live without the weight of anyone else's expectations.

But lately, something's been shifting. Maybe it's watching my sisters build these rich, full lives, or maybe it's just the accumulation of years and injuries that make me wonder what comes next. My body won't be able to handle stunts forever, and then what? The family business starts to look less like a safety net and more like an inevitability.

The resistance to settling down isn't about not wanting love; it's about trusting the person. And it's just easier to keep things light, fun, uncomplicated with the type of work I do. Everyone knows where they stand, no one gets hurt, and I get to keep being the charming guy who's great for a good time but not for the long haul.

My phone buzzes with a text.

GIULIANA

Don't let them get to you. You'll figure it out when you're ready.

I'm typing back a thank-you when I hear the familiar sound of a key in my lock, followed by a voice that always makes me smile.

"Knock, knock," Stella calls out as the door opens. "Hope you're decent."

"Decent enough," I call back, closing my laptop and standing up to greet her.

She appears in my living room, carrying a takeout container and looking slightly flushed from what I'm guessing was one of her yoga classes with Natalie. She's in leggings and an oversized sweatshirt, her blonde hair pulled back in a messy ponytail, and there's something about the casual comfort of her presence that immediately settles the restless energy left over from the family call.

"Avocado bacon Benedict from that place across from the yoga studio," she announces, holding up the container like a peace offering. "Figured you probably haven't eaten anything real today."

"You figured right," I admit, accepting the food gratefully. "How'd you know I needed this?"

"You always want food." She studies my expression with the kind of perceptive attention that makes me wonder sometimes how she reads people so well. "You have that post-family-call look on your face. Everyone still trying to run your life from three thousand miles away?"

"Something like that." I settle back onto the couch and gesture for her to join me. "Want to split this? It's huge."

"I already ate with Natalie, but thanks." She perches on the edge of the coffee table instead, close enough that I can smell her perfume mixed with the faint scent of her sweat. "Everything okay, though? You look a little..."

"Contemplative?"

"I was going to say brooding, but contemplative works, too."

I fork a bite of the Benedict, which is absolutely perfect, and consider how much to share. Stella and I have an easy friendship that comes with the kind of comfortable honesty and no expectations of each other. She's safe to talk to, partly because she's not trying to fix me or change me and partly because she's dealing with her own complicated feelings about life and love. But mostly, it's because she's never once looked at me and seen dollar signs or opportunities.

When she looks at me, she sees someone worth her time and attention. Someone whose opinion matters to her, whose stories she actually listens to and whose dreams she takes seriously. She challenges me to think bigger about my career, celebrates my wins like they're her own, and never makes me feel like I need to be anything other than exactly who I am. There's something freeing about that kind of trust.

"Just family stuff," I say finally. "They want me to think about the future."

"Ah. The dreaded 'what's your five-year plan' conversation."

"More like the 'when are you going to give us grandchildren and join the family business' conversation."

Stella nods knowingly. "I get versions of that call, too. Different content, same underlying message." She checks her phone and stands. "Hang in there and don't worry too much. I'll let you eat in peace, I've got to return some email."

"Thanks for this," I say, holding up the container. "And for checking on me."

"Anytime." She heads toward the door, then pauses and turns back. "Hey, Brandon?"

"Yeah?"

"For what it's worth, I think you're exactly where you're supposed to be right now. You've got plenty of time to figure out exactly what you want."

six

· · ·

Stella

I'M deep in a Google rabbit hole about Mason Park when my phone rings. The screen shows a photo of my mother in her perfectly coordinated tennis outfit, her blonde hair in a flawless bob, holding a martini at last year's charity gala.

I steel myself for the conversation and answer on the third ring.

"Hey, Mama."

"Stella Suzanne, darling! How are you, sweet pea?"

Her voice carries that particular blend of warmth and expectation that I've been hearing my entire life. I can picture her exactly, probably sitting in the sunroom with her morning coffee and already dressed for whatever committee meeting or charity luncheon is on today's agenda.

"I'm good. Just getting settled at the office." I glance around the agency, grateful that Blair's on maternity leave and can't overhear this conversation.

"Oh, good, you're not too busy, then. I wanted to catch you before your day gets away from you." There's a pause, and I brace myself. "Honey, did you ever reach out to Patricia Wrigley's son? You remember, I texted you his number the other day. He just moved out to Los Angeles for work. Such a lovely boy, just finished his MBA at Emory. I thought you could reach out, maybe show him around town, help him get settled."

I close my eyes. Patricia Wrigley's son. Right. The latest in my mother's endless parade of "perfect matches" for me.

"I've been really swamped with work, Mama."

"Stella, darling, work is wonderful, but it shouldn't consume your whole life. You're twenty-five. When I was your age, I was already married to your father and planning our family."

Here we go.

I fidget with my pen, drawing little stars on my notepad.

"I know, but things are different nowadays. And I love what I do here."

"And I'm proud of you, sugar; you know that. But this whole Hollywood thing..." She sighs dramatically. "I just worry you're missing out on what really matters. Building a life, a family. Finding a good man who can take care of you."

"I can take care of myself."

"Of course you can, but why should you have to? And I'm still holding out hope that you'll move back home. You could join the Junior League with me like we always planned. I could get you on the hospital auxiliary board tomorrow."

The familiar weight of obligation settles on my chest. In her mind, my life in LA is still just an extended vacation, a wild phase I'll eventually outgrow when I remember what really matters.

"Actually, Mama, I'm seeing someone." The words tumble out before I can stop them.

There's a beat of silence, then a sharp intake of breath. "You are? Oh, honey! Why didn't you tell me? Who is he? What does he do?"

"Still early days," I say, hoping my voice sounds breezy instead of panicked. "I don't want to jinx it."

"Oh, sweetheart, I'm so excited for you!" Her voice is practically glowing through the phone. "You know what? I'm going to go ahead and mark you down as having a plus-one for the summer charity gala. It would be the perfect opportunity for you to introduce him."

I can hear the hope in her voice, the way she's already mentally planning introductions and probably picking out what she'll wear to meet my mystery boyfriend. Part of me feels guilty for the deception, but a bigger part feels relief at how this buys me some breathing room.

"That sounds lovely, Mama," I say because it's easier than explaining that my dating life is currently a figment of my imagination.

"I just have such a good feeling about this, baby girl. I can tell in your voice that this one might be special." She sighs happily. "I can't wait to see you happy and settled."

"Let's not get ahead of ourselves."

"Well, if it doesn't work out, I can make sure Patricia's son can escort you. I do think he'd be a good match for you, too."

I hum something that could pass for agreement and let her enthusiasm wash over me. At least now I have a little time to figure out my life.

"Okay, Mama. I need to get back to work."

We chat for a few more minutes about the luncheon she's headed to today and Daddy's golf game before she finally lets me go.

My pulse flutters wildly as the reality of what I told her hits me. I'm dating someone. My stomach churns with a nauseating mix of anxiety and regret as I realize the magnitude of the lie I just told.

I pull out my phone with shaking hands, my leg bouncing uncontrollably under my desk as I try to formulate a coherent cry for help. How do I even begin to explain this disaster? My fingers hover over the keyboard, typing and deleting the same words three times before I finally manage to hit send on my SOS message to the Girl Gang.

STELLA

Soooo. I have a little issue.

SOPHIA

What happened? Are you okay?

JESS

Do we need to hide a body?

NATALIE

I have bail money if needed.

STELLA

Well. I just told my mother I'm dating someone so she'd stop pushing blind dates on me. Now she expects me to bring him as my plus-one to the charity gala we attend every summer.

BRANDON

Why would you do that?

NATALIE

Honestly? Kind of proud. Fake it till you make it, girl.

JESS

Wait, so you're not dating anyone?

STELLA

Correct. Desperately single. But now I need a date or boyfriend or both. Unless I want to be set up with one of her friend's sons.

BLAIR

Just catching up. I was nursing little Ruby. I have the cutest baby in my arms right now!

SOPHIA

OMG, pics please! Auntie Sophia requires proof of life.

BLAIR

[shared baby Ruby photo album]

JESS

Stop it right now. She's perfect. I'm crying actual tears.

STELLA

Blair, she's absolutely gorgeous! Look at those tiny fingers!

BRANDON

That's one beautiful baby. Congratulations again.

NATALIE

Okay wow, she's stunning. Those cheeks!

SOPHIA

I'M DEAD. Look at that face! When can I come see her again?

BLAIR

Thank you 🩶 I'm going to plan a get-together for all of us soon. But let's get back to Stella's problem. I can tell this is about to get entertaining.

STELLA

If by entertaining you mean becoming an absolute dumpster fire. So, anyone have any single friends?

SOPHIA

I can look through my contacts. I'm sure I know a ton of single guys.

BRANDON

No way, Sophia. The guys you know are arrogant assholes.

SOPHIA

Hey! Not all of them!

NATALIE

Say no more. We've got your back.

JESS

I'm an excellent matchmaker.

STELLA

I appreciate any ideas you all have.

NATALIE

Want to grab lunch and discuss on Sunday?

STELLA

If that works for everyone, I can host and I'll feed you for your troubles.

SOPHIA

I'll be there!

BRANDON

Why are we doing this again?

NATALIE

I feel like it's obvious.

JESS

I'll be there too.

BLAIR

Can you FaceTime me in? I don't want to
miss this.

I set my phone down and stare at my computer screen. Despite the panic, I'm a little excited at the idea of my friends helping me get back out there. Who knows? Maybe I'll actually find a love connection.

seven

. . .

Stella

I'M PUTTING the finishing touches on a charcuterie board when my friends start arriving for what we're calling our Sunday matchmaking session. It's basically "help Stella get back into dating so she has options for the gala," which sounds much more reasonable when I put it that way.

"You always make the best boards," Natalie says, settling onto my couch with her usual grace and immediately reaching for the brie.

"I figured if I'm going to ask you all to play matchmaker, the least I can do is feed you properly," I say, arranging crackers around the cheese.

Jess arrives with her laptop, because of course she does. "I may have already started a preliminary list of eligible bachelors."

"You work fast," Sophia laughs, claiming the chair by the window. "I love it."

Brandon settles onto the opposite end of the couch from

Natalie, looking skeptical. "I still don't understand why you can't just tell your mom you'll find someone when you're ready. Why the performance?"

"Because you don't know my mother," I say, pouring wine. "She's been in matchmaking mode my entire life. She probably had my wedding planned before I could walk. This buys me some breathing room."

"Plus," Natalie adds, "maybe we'll actually find her someone great. Win-win."

Blair appears on Sophia's laptop screen, with baby Ruby visible in her arms. "Sorry I'm late! Feeding time. But I'm here for moral support and terrible dating advice."

I settle cross-legged on the floor, wine in hand. "Okay, so here's the situation. I told my mom I'm seeing someone to get her off my back about blind dates. Now she's expecting me to bring him to their summer charity gala."

"What kind of guy are you even looking for?" Jess asks, her fingers poised over her keyboard.

I pause, realizing I haven't actually thought about this in concrete terms. "I don't know. Someone nice? Funny? Employed?"

"Stella," Sophia says gently, "you've got to give us more than that. What's your type?"

"I honestly don't know if I have one," I admit. "I've only had two serious boyfriends. My high school boyfriend was basically my mother's pick and lasted through most of college. Then there was a marketing guy I dated briefly last year who was perfectly fine but boring as toast."

Brandon raises an eyebrow. "That's it? Two?"

"I've been focused on my career," I say with a laugh. "Plus, not all of us have your extensive experience in the romance department."

"No judgment," Jess says quickly. "Just trying to understand what we're working with. Do you want someone in the industry? Outside it? Creative type? Business guy?"

I think about it, swirling my wine. "Maybe someone who gets that my job is important to me? Who doesn't expect me to be available twenty-four-seven or think my career is just a cute hobby until I get married?"

"Reasonable standard," Blair says from the laptop. "What else?"

"Someone who makes me laugh. Someone I can actually talk to." I pause. "Someone who doesn't make me feel like I need to be a different version of myself."

There's something about the way Brandon is looking at me that makes me add, "And, obviously, someone my parents would think is a good match, since that's kind of the point."

Brandon just nods, but I catch something shift in his expression before he takes a sip of his wine.

"What about that Mason guy?" Natalie asks, her eyes sparkling.

My stomach drops. "I wish. He's... No."

"Why not?" Jess demands. "He's cute. And he seems normal."

Sophia nods. "And he lives in the building, easy to run into."

I chew my lip, embarrassed to even say it out loud. "Because every time I see him, my brain short-circuits. He's a little out of my league."

"Correction," Brandon cuts in, his voice steady. "He's not out of your league, sunshine. Your out of his."

The room falls quiet for a beat. My cheeks heat, and I look away, grabbing a cheese cube like it might save me.

"Stell," Jess says, incredulous. "You're smart, gorgeous, and kind. A total catch."

I laugh, but it comes out a little brittle. "You don't get it. I grew up thinking the only way to land a guy was to be perfect. Smile just enough, never eat more than half your entrée, don't be too loud, don't be too quiet. My mom literally has a checklist."

Natalie groans. "Gross."

Sophia leans forward, determined. "Then we need to un-checklist you. The right guy is going to like you for *you*, not some Stepford version."

"Newsflash, Rhodes: you're already a catch," Brandon says. "If some guy can't see that, he's the problem, not you." His voice is casual, but it cuts right through me.

I glance at him, and something warm stirs in my chest. He's looking at me like it's the most obvious fact in the world. Then, before I can respond, he's up and in my kitchen to make some popcorn like he didn't just pay me one of the best compliments of my life.

Blair clears her throat. "Alright, so, let's talk options. Bars or clubs, volunteering, coffee shops—where are we sending Stella to meet eligible men?"

Ideas start flying. Natalie suggests yoga classes. Sophia brings up a studio premiere. Jess proposes speed dating, to which I immediately say absolutely not. Brandon mutters something about "making sure these guys can string a sentence together."

Within twenty minutes, Jess has a color-coded calendar on her laptop, with everyone pitching touchpoints where I might naturally cross paths with someone decent.

I exhale, half overwhelmed, half relieved. "Okay. Now all I need are tips on how to be the girl that guys want to date."

Brandon nudges a wineglass toward me. "Or you could just be yourself and see who's smart enough to notice."

The words should be reassuring, but instead, they make my stomach twist with familiar anxiety. Be myself. Right. Only myself is the girl who freezes up around attractive men, who overthinks every conversation until it becomes weird, who somehow transforms from competent talent agent to bumbling mess the second romance enters the picture. It's like there are two versions of me—the one who can negotiate million-dollar deals without breaking a sweat and the one who can't figure out how to flirt without feeling like I'm performing some role I never learned properly.

I know my friends see the confident version and can't understand why I'm so insecure about dating, but they don't see how I second-guess every word, every outfit, every text message. They don't know that I spend hours wondering if I'm pretty enough, funny enough, interesting enough to hold someone's attention beyond a first date.

"Easy for you to say," I tell Brandon, forcing a smile. "You don't turn into a completely different person the second you're attracted to someone."

He gives me a look that I can't decipher and stands to grab another drink. "Noted."

By the time the conversation winds down, my living room looks a bit like a war room with plates scattered around and sticky notes everywhere. I walk everyone to the door with promises of updates, and when I turn back, Brandon's still inside, gathering stray glasses.

My hands twist together in front of me as I move across the apartment to where he stands in my kitchen. "Can I ask you something?"

He glances over. "Shoot."

"How do you do it? You always seem to have a girlfriend, or at least someone interested. It's easy for you."

He leans a hip against the counter, turning fully toward me like he's actually going to take the question seriously. "If I were going to offer a suggestion..."

"Yes?"

"Confidence is sexy, Stella. Even if you're faking it at first." His tone is matter-of-fact, like he's pointing out the sky is blue. "You have to believe you're worth the attention."

The words land heavier than I expect, sliding past my practiced smile and straight into the hollow spot I usually ignore.

I fold my arms, more to steady myself than to challenge him. "Easier said than done."

He studies me for a moment, not with pity but with something steadier, something that makes my chest go tight. Then he gives me that grin—the easy, maddeningly confident one I've seen him use to charm waitresses and casting assistants alike. Only, this time, it feels like it's just for me.

"That's why you practice," he says softly. "Start with someone who already knows you're worth it."

I swallow and force a laugh to break the tension. "You volunteering as tribute, Grimaldi?"

His smile tilts, playful again. "Depends on what the job description looks like."

It's the second time he's mentioned helping me. And I think I'm going to take him up on it.

eight

. . .

Brandon

I SIT in the sterile examination room, trying not to fidget as Dr. Cohen reviews my chart. The paper crinkles under me every time I shift on the table, and the fluorescent lights over-head make everything feel harsh and clinical. Not exactly the ideal setting I was going for today.

"So, Brandon," he says, looking up with that easy smile that's made him my go-to doctor for the past five years. "I finally saw the *Roadhouse* remake. That bar fight sequence was incredible. How many takes did that final throw take?"

I grin, relaxing slightly. "Seven. The first six, I kept landing about two inches off my mark."

"Jesus." Shaking his head, he makes notes on his tablet. "I don't know how you do it. I get winded walking up two flights of stairs."

"Practice and a very expensive chiropractor," I say, rolling my shoulders experimentally. The left one gives a small protest, like it always does these days, but nothing dramatic. "Speaking of which, this should be pretty routine today, right? I've got a Marvel audition coming up, and they need the physical submitted pretty soon."

"Should be." He sets down his tablet and pulls on latex gloves. "Let's start with the basics and see how everything looks."

The first part goes exactly as expected. Blood pressure, heart rate, reflexes—all the standard stuff that's never given me trouble. Dr. Cohen makes small talk about my work, asking questions that make me think he's actually interested in what I do instead of just being polite.

"I always wondered how you guys make those falls look so real without actually getting hurt," he says while checking my reflexes with that little rubber hammer.

"It's all about angles and timing. Plus knowing exactly where to land and how to—" I stop mid-sentence as he moves to test my left shoulder. Something feels wrong the moment he starts manipulating the joint. "Huh."

"What?"

"Nothing, just...that felt different than usual."

Dr. Cohen's expression shifts slightly, becoming more focused. "Can you lift your arm straight up for me?"

I do and immediately feel that familiar catch at about ninety degrees. It's been there for months, ever since the accident on the Caldwell project, but it's manageable. Or so I thought.

"Now rotate it backward. Slowly."

The movement sends a sharp twinge down my arm, and I can't quite suppress the small grunt of discomfort. The doctor's hands are gentle but thorough as he manipulates the joint, testing the range of motion, checking for instability.

"When was your last MRI on this shoulder?"

"Right after the injury. Maybe a year ago?" My stomach starts to clench. "Why?"

Instead of answering immediately, he has me do a series of movements that has me reaching overhead, behind my back, and across my chest. Each one reveals limitations I've been unconsciously working around for weeks. By the time he's finished, his expression is carefully neutral in the way doctors get when they're about to deliver news you don't want to hear.

"I'm going to be straight with you," he says, pulling off his gloves and settling onto his rolling stool. "I can't clear you for physical activity right now."

The words hit me like a physical blow. "What do you mean?"

"Your shoulder mobility is significantly compromised from where it was six months ago. You're compensating in ways that are putting strain on other muscle groups."

I stare at him, trying to process what he's saying. "But I feel fine. I mean, it's a little stiff, but I've been working through it. I just finished a whole fight scene last week without any problems."

"You've been managing it, which is different than it being healed." He pulls up something on his tablet and shows me what looks like notes from previous visits. "Your range of motion has decreased by thirty percent since your last physical. That's not normal recovery; that's regression."

The room feels like it's getting smaller. "So, what are you saying? That I can't do stunts anymore?"

"I'm saying you need proper physical therapy and probably another MRI to see what's going on structurally. Give it three months of dedicated rehab, then come back, and we'll reassess." His expression softens slightly. "Brandon, you're thirty-two. Your body doesn't bounce back the way it used to. That doesn't mean your career is over, but it might mean it's time to think about what comes next."

Three months. The Marvel project starts filming in six weeks. By the time I'm cleared—if I'm cleared—they'll already have hired someone else. Someone younger, someone whose body hasn't started betraying them in the middle of what should be the biggest opportunity of my career.

"What about my current project?" I ask, with panic starting to creep into my voice. "I'm already booked through next month."

"As long as you're not doing anything that aggravates the shoulder, you should be fine to finish out existing commitments. But no new bookings until we get this sorted out."

The relief is small but significant. At least I won't have to explain to anyone why I'm suddenly backing out of work. But the bigger picture is terrifying. If I can't do stunts anymore, what the hell am I supposed to do with my life?

I slide off the examination table. My legs feel unsteady underneath me. "Yeah, okay."

"Brandon, listen to me. This isn't the end of the world. With proper treatment, there's every reason to believe you'll be back to full capacity in a few months."

He's trying to be encouraging, but all I can hear is the sound of the door closing on my career. A reminder that this career I've built won't last forever.

"Can you recommend someone for the PT?" I ask

because I need to do something productive with this conversation before I lose it completely.

"Absolutely. I'll send you a referral today." He pauses, studying my face. "And Brandon? Take this seriously. Don't try to push through it or work around it. Your body is telling you something important."

I nod, not trusting my voice, and shake his hand before heading for the door. The hallway feels endless as I walk toward the exit, my mind racing through all the implications of what just happened.

I make it to my car before the real panic hits. Sitting in the parking garage, staring at the concrete wall in front of me, I feel every one of my thirty-two years pressing down on my shoulders. If I can't do stunts anymore, what am I supposed to do? Go crawling back to New York with my tail between my legs, admit that my family might have been right about this being an unsustainable career? Start managing luxury resorts like Dad's been hinting at for years?

The thought makes my stomach turn. I love what I do. I love the adrenaline, the precision, the way every day is different. I love being part of something bigger than myself, helping tell stories that matter. The idea of trading all that for spreadsheets and guest satisfaction surveys feels like giving up everything that makes me who I am.

My phone buzzes with a text, and for a moment, my heart sinks, thinking it might be work related. But it's from Stella.

STELLA

I'm running behind tonight so probably
won't be there until 8pm.

The simple message hits me differently than it usually would. Suddenly, the thought of sitting on her couch feels like a safe space to process this day. Not because I want to talk about what just happened—I'm nowhere near ready for that conversation—but because Stella's apartment feels like the one place where I can just exist without having to perform or prove anything.

BRANDON

Ok, want me to grab food?

STELLA

You can bring wine. I've got dinner covered.

I thumbs up the text, then start the car and head back to the studio for a few more hours, already feeling some of the tension in my chest beginning to ease. Whatever happens with my career, whatever decisions I have to make in the coming months, at least I have good friends I can lean on if I need to.

nine

. . .

Brandon

I **LET** myself into Stella's apartment right at eight, bottle of wine in hand, trying to shut down the loop still playing in my head from earlier.

I can't clear you for physical activity right now. Your shoulder mobility is significantly compromised from where it was six months ago.

Dr. Cohen might as well have stapled the words to my forehead.

Inside, Stella's already padding across the hardwood floor in an oversized USC sweatshirt and a pair of cotton shorts, her blonde hair twisted up in one of those messy buns that look effortless.

She lights up when she sees the wine. "You brought Cakebread? You do love me!"

She grabs the food from the kitchen and heads to the couch. "I've got *Love Island* queued up. Tonight's the bombshell drop. I have so many theories."

Her apartment smells faintly like eucalyptus and citrus

from a diffuser that sits on the entry table, and her apartment has become a sense of familiar comfort over the past few months. Her décor is inspired by her Southern roots, with clean lines, soft tones, and fresh flowers on the coffee table. The windowsill, however, is a nod to LA. It's lined with tiny crystals that she insists keep her energy grounded. The couch is half-buried in throw pillows that defy physics and comfort, but somehow, this place always feels like a soft landing.

I drop into my usual spot on the right side of the sectional and settle with my head at one end and feet at the other while she plates our dinner.

We've been doing this Thursday night thing for, man, I guess around six months now. Ever since Jess moved out after accidentally marrying Lucas in Vegas and deciding to *stay* married.

Stella took over her lease, and that's how I ended up with a standing appointment to eat takeout on her couch and watch hot people in swimwear make terrible decisions.

"Okay, so, before we start," she says, settling next to me with her legs tucked under her, "I need to tell you my prediction about what's going to happen with Coco and Warren."

"You always have predictions," I say, but I'm smiling. This is peak Stella, analyzing reality TV like it's Shakespeare.

She points her fork at me. "And I'm usually right. Remember when I called that Miles was going to choose Ellie over Maycie three episodes before it happened?"

"Lucky guess."

"Intuition," she corrects. "It's all about reading body language and understanding what people really want versus what they think they want."

I study her face, genuinely curious about this disconnect I've always noticed. "So, you can read everyone else like a book, but when it comes to yourself..."

"I'm completely blind," she finishes with a self-deprecating laugh. "When it's about other people, I can see everything clearly. But the second it involves me—what I want, what I'm good at, whether someone's actually interested—my brain just shuts down. All that intuition disappears."

It's fascinating, really. Stella can walk into a room and immediately assess the power dynamics, figure out who's insecure, who's putting on an act, who's genuinely confident. She can spot a fake smile from across a party. But ask her to evaluate her own worth or recognize when someone's flirting with her, and she's completely lost.

Maybe it's because she's been told what she should want for so long that she's forgotten how to trust what she actually feels. Or maybe it's easier to analyze other people's lives because there's no risk involved. She can be more objective when her own heart isn't on the line.

She hits play and immediately pauses again when the first couple appears on screen. "See? Look at how he's standing. His feet are pointed toward the door, not toward her. Classic subconscious signal that he wants to escape."

I try to focus on her commentary, but Dr. Cohen's voice keeps cutting through. Three months of physical therapy. Three months of hoping my shoulder decides to cooperate. Three months of pretending everything's fine while I watch other guys audition for jobs I should be going after.

"Brandon?" Stella's voice pulls me back. She's paused the

show again and is looking at me with those blue eyes that miss nothing. "You're not even watching. What's going on?"

I consider brushing it off, making some joke about being distracted by her excellent analysis skills. But this is Stella. She's the one person I trust completely. If I can't tell her, who can I tell?

"I had my physical today," I say, setting down my food.

"And?" She mutes the TV completely, giving me her full attention.

"And I didn't pass." The words taste bitter. "My shoulder's not where it needs to be. Doc won't clear me for any new work and is making me return to physical therapy."

Her face immediately softens. "Oh, Brandon."

"Three months," I continue because, if I stop talking, I might actually lose it. "Three months of physical therapy, and then I can retest. But it means I can't go after the Marvel gig. And if the production I'm on now finds out I'm not cleared..." I trail off, but we both know how this story ends. They'll replace me faster than I can say "stunt double."

Stella sets down her own food and turns to face me completely. "How are you feeling about it?"

Leave it to Stella to ask the real question instead of offering empty reassurances. It's one of the things I love about her, this ability to cut straight to the heart of things.

"Terrified," I admit. "This is all I know how to do, Stella. I've been doing stunts for fourteen years. If my body can't handle it anymore..."

"Then you transition. There are a million other things you could do in this space," she says simply. "You're one of the most talented stunt actors I've ever seen work, but you are so much more than that. Remember that fight scene you choreographed for Sophia's last film? It was incredible."

"That's different."

"Is it? You'd still be in the industry you love, still doing work that matters. Just because you're not the one getting thrown through windows doesn't mean you wouldn't be valuable."

I want to believe her, but there's this voice in my head that sounds suspiciously like my father, suggesting there's more to work. I'll admit, what he was suggesting sounded nice for a minute. Like maybe there is something more in life to want than just a career.

"What if coordinating isn't enough?" I ask. "What if my family's right and I should just join the family business, work at the hotels like everyone else?"

"Are you kidding me?" Stella's voice is sharp with disbelief. "Brandon, you've built an incredible career doing what you love. You don't have to quit what you love for the family business."

"Will you keep this between us for now?" I ask. "I need time to figure out my next move."

"Of course." She reaches over and squeezes my hand. "But Brandon, I want to help. This is what I do for clients all the time. Career planning, positioning for transitions. Let me help you figure out your next steps."

The relief that washes over me is immediate. This is why Stella's so good at her job. She doesn't just see what people are—she sees what they could become.

"Thank you," I say, and I mean it. "Seriously, Stell. I don't know what I'd do without you."

She smiles at me over her glass, then hesitates. "Okay, well...if you really want to return the favor..."

I raise an eyebrow. "Uh-oh."

She laughs. "It's not a big deal. I know we've been joking about you giving me lessons, but..."

I wait.

"Look at how I act around Mason," she says, picking at the edge of a napkin. "I keep freezing every time he talks to me. But it's not just him; it's every guy."

A sly grin creeps across my face. "You want me to teach you to flirt?"

"I don't need to *flirt*," she says a little too quickly. "Well, okay. Maybe I need to learn that, too. But all the stuff that comes after that. How can I get his attention and talk to him so he'll actually ask me out?"

"Stella, you don't need help with that," I say carefully. "Trust me. Any guy would be lucky to get your attention."

She waves off my compliment like she always does. "You have to say that. You're my friend. But clearly, I'm missing something. Look at these girls." She gestures at the paused TV screen, where some reality show contestant is lounging by a pool in a bikini. "They know how to get guys interested. They're confident, sexy, flirty."

"You're all of those things."

"No, I'm polite. There's a difference." She grabs the remote and fast-forwards to a scene where one of the women is clearly trying to seduce someone. "See? Look at how she moves, how she talks to him. It's like she knows she's irresistible."

I watch the screen, then look back at Stella, who's

studying the interaction like she's preparing for a business presentation.

"You want to act like that?" I ask.

"Why not? If it works..." She stands suddenly and pulls her sweatshirt over her head, revealing a black sports bra underneath. "I do this, right? Because boobs. You have to see them. I know guys like that."

What the fuck is happening right now?

Why is Stella taking off her shirt? She's completely comfortable, like this is the most natural thing in the world, and I'm trying very hard not to notice that she has a really great... Focus, Brandon.

"You're always saying confidence is sexy," she continues, and before I can process what's happening, she's climbing onto the sectional, moving up from where my feet were to where I'm lying, settling between my legs with that analytical expression still on her face. "So, something like this would be hot, right?"

I swallow hard. She's close enough that I can see the determination in her eyes, the way she's treating this like a business problem to solve. Which should not be as attractive as it is.

"You basically just narrate everything you're doing, right?" she says, her voice dropping to that purr again. "Your chest is so hard and smooth." Her palm slides up my t-shirt, and I feel my breath catch. "And I love the way my fingers feel running through your hair." Her fingertips graze my scalp, sending electricity straight down my spine. "And your lips."

When her thumb brushes across my mouth, every

coherent thought I've ever had evaporates. I grab her hand before I do something monumentally stupid.

"Okay, yes, I get the idea," I manage, my voice rougher than it should be. "See? You don't need any help at all."

She sits back on her heels, still between my legs, completely oblivious to the fact that she just short-circuited my brain and made me semi-hard.

"Yeah, but I wouldn't be that comfortable with anyone else," she says matter-of-factly. "I can't even talk to guys without freezing up."

I fucking love the idea that she's comfortable doing that with me, but I stare at her for a long moment, wondering if she has any idea what she just did to me. The answer is clearly no because she's looking at me with those big blue eyes like I'm her favorite person in the world and she trusts me completely.

Which makes me the worst friend ever for the thoughts I'm currently having.

"Fine," I say because apparently I'm a masochist. "I'll help you."

What could possibly go wrong?

ten

. . .

Stella

"YOU'RE REALLY GOING to help me?" I bounce slightly on my couch cushions, barely able to contain my excitement. "Thank you, thank you! I actually started a list."

Brandon's still looking at me with that slightly dazed expression he's been wearing since I demonstrated what I thought flirting looked like. His cheeks are flushed, and he keeps running his hand through his hair like he's trying to reset his brain.

"Yeah," he says, his voice rougher than usual. "I mean, you don't really need help, but if you want pointers on how to be more...confident, I can work with that."

I grab my food and settle cross-legged, facing him. "So, what's lesson one? Eye contact? Body language? Should I take notes?"

"Stella, you don't need to—"

A sharp knock at my door cuts him off mid-sentence. We both freeze, staring at each other like we've been caught doing something illegal.

"Are you expecting someone?" Brandon asks quietly.

I shake my head. It's eight-thirty on a Thursday night. Blair's home with the baby, Jess and Lucas are at some industry event, and Natalie teaches evening yoga classes. Nobody just drops by unannounced.

The knock comes again, followed by a familiar voice that makes my blood turn to ice water.

"Stella Suzanne? Sugar, are you home? I can hear the television."

"Oh, my God," I whisper, scrambling off the couch so fast I nearly knock over my wine glass. "That's my mother."

Brandon's eyebrows shoot up. "Your mother? From Georgia? What is she doing here?"

"I have absolutely no idea." I'm smoothing down my hair and glancing around my apartment like it's been hit by a tornado instead of just containing evidence of our usual Thursday night routine. "Just...stay here and be cool. She's harmless, I promise."

I open the door to find my mother standing in the hallway, wearing a cream-colored pantsuit and her blonde hair in a perfect bob despite what must have been hours of travel. She's holding a designer handbag and a small rolling suitcase, and the moment she sees me, her face lights up like it's Christmas morning.

"Surprise, baby girl!" She pulls me into a hug that smells like Chanel No. 5 and home, squeezing me tight before pulling back to examine my face.

"Mama, what are you doing here?"

"I couldn't wait another minute to meet this mystery boyfriend you've been keeping from us."

"What?" The blood rushes from my face, and I must look like a ghost. In fact, I think I'm going to pass out.

"Well, when you told me you were seeing someone, I just got so excited." She's already looking past me into my apartment, her sharp eyes taking inventory. "Your father's at some tedious golf tournament in Hilton Head, so I thought, why not fly out now and have some mother-daughter time? And maybe meet the man who's captured my baby's heart."

Her gaze lands on Brandon, who's standing frozen by my coffee table like a deer caught in headlights. He's still holding his plate of food, his hair is mussed from running his hands through it, and he looks like he'd rather be anywhere else in the world.

"Oh, my stars!" she gasps, pressing a hand to her chest, and then whispers, "Is this him? Stella Suzanne, you didn't tell me he was so handsome!"

My brain short-circuits completely. This is it. This is the moment where I either confess that I'm a pathological liar who invented a boyfriend to avoid blind dates or I figure out some way to salvage this disaster. My mother is staring at Brandon with the kind of delighted expression she usually reserves for babies and wedding announcements, and he looks like he's about to bolt for the door. I need to say something. Anything. But what comes out of my mouth is somehow both the worst possible option and my only way out of this mess.

"Mama, this is Brandon," I say, my voice getting higher with each word. "Brandon Grimaldi. My boyfriend. He lives across the hall. So convenient to have a boyfriend so nearby."

Oh, God. Oh, no. What am I doing? I just called

Brandon my boyfriend. To my mother. Out loud. There's no taking this back now.

I can't seem to stop talking; the words tumble out of my mouth like I've lost all control over my vocal cords. I'm too terrified to look at Brandon directly, so I shift my eyes sideways without turning my head. I can see him staring at me, and I'm pretty sure those are the whites of his eyes taking up most of his face.

Please play along, I pray silently.

"Hello, Brandon!" my mother exclaims, rushing toward him with her arms outstretched. "It's so nice to meet you!"

She pulls him into one of her signature Southern mama hugs, and over her shoulder, Brandon shoots me a look that could absolutely be classified as murderous. I bring my hands up in a desperate pleading gesture, and his eyes narrow in a way that tells me I'm going to be buying our Thursday night dinners for the next year.

When she finally releases him, something magical happens. Brandon's entire demeanor shifts, and suddenly, he's all charm and grace. Even I'm convinced we're dating.

"Mrs. Rhodes, it's such a pleasure to meet you," he says, his voice warm and smooth. "I can see where Stella gets her beauty."

My mother practically melts on the spot.

"And I have to tell you," he continues, reaching over to take my hand and pull me against his side, "I absolutely adore your daughter. She's the most incredible woman I've ever met."

Holy shit. He's actually doing it. He's holding my hand

and telling my mother he adores me with the kind of sincerity that could win him an Oscar. I can literally see her falling for it in real time.

The casual way he touches me, like it's the most natural thing in the world, sends an unexpected flutter through my stomach. Even knowing this is all an act, my skin tingles where his fingers brush against mine.

"Please, call me Caroline. And what do you do, Brandon? Besides sweep my daughter off her feet, apparently."

"I'm a stuntman," he says simply. "I work in film and television."

My mother's eyebrows shoot up, but instead of the disapproval I'm expecting, she looks impressed. "A stuntman! How exciting. That must require incredible strength and athleticism."

"It has its moments," Brandon says, shooting me a glance that clearly asks, "Is this really happening?"

"So, how long have you two been seeing each other?" she asks, her eyes bright with curiosity.

"Not long," I say quickly. "Like I told you, it's still really new."

"But promising," my mother says with a knowing smile. "I can tell. You have that glow, sugar."

Brandon clears his throat. "So, uh, how long are you planning to visit?"

"Oh, just a few days." She gestures to the rolling bag in the hallway. "I thought I could stay in your guest room and we could have some lovely mother-daughter time. And of course, I want to get to know Brandon better."

My guest room. Which doesn't exist. Because I live in a one-bedroom apartment with a living room, kitchen, and bathroom. There is no guest room.

"Actually, Mama, I don't have a guest room. This is just a one-bedroom."

She gets a perplexed look on her face, one that makes her look like she already knew that detail, and immediately, I'm suspicious. "Oh. Well, that's fine. I can take the couch. I'm not picky."

Crap on a cracker. I can't let my mother sleep on the couch. "Mama, you can't sleep on that. You'll hurt your back."

"Then where do you suggest I stay? A hotel?"

Yes. Yes, I do. She loves fancy hotels. I'm not sure where she's going with this. Her acting skills escalate to look offended, like staying in a hotel is the equivalent of sleeping in a cardboard box.

And that's when my mother's gaze shifts between Brandon and me, and I can practically see the gears turning in her head. Her eyes narrow slightly as she takes in the dinner setup, the way we're standing close together, the general domestic comfort of the scene.

"Unless..." she says slowly as a knowing smile creeps across her face. "Unless you two are already staying together most of the time anyway?"

My face goes completely red. "Mama!"

"Oh, don't be embarrassed, sugar. I'm a modern woman. I know how these things work." She waves a hand dismissively. "Young couples spend time at each other's places. It's perfectly natural."

Brandon looks like he's having an out-of-body experience. "We're not... I mean, we don't..."

"That's right," I jump in, my voice pitched about an octave higher than normal. "What I mean is, I usually stay at his place. Because it's bigger. And has a better...shower."

The lies are just pouring out of me now, each one digging the hole deeper. Brandon's staring at me like I've lost my mind, which I probably have.

"Perfect!" my mother exclaims, clapping her hands together. "Then I'll just stay here in Stella's apartment for a few days, and you two can continue your normal routine at Brandon's place. Problem solved!"

The room goes completely silent. I can hear the air conditioning humming, the distant sound of traffic outside, the rapid beating of my own heart as the full magnitude of what just happened hits me.

"That's..." I have absolutely no idea how to finish that sentence.

"Wonderful," Brandon says faintly, though he looks anything but convinced. "Just...wonderful."

"Well, it was lovely to meet you, Brandon, but I'm absolutely exhausted. All that traveling has worn me out," my mother says, settling onto my couch like she owns the place. "Don't let me keep you from your evening plans. I'm sure you two want to get back to Brandon's place and get settled."

She's looking at us expectantly, clearly waiting for us to pack up and leave so she can take over my apartment.

"Right," I say weakly. "We should...go do that. Get settled."

Brandon nods slowly, his charm starting to slip. "Settled. At my place. Where we...usually stay. Together."

"How sweet," my mother coos. "Young love is just so precious."

And that's how Brandon Grimaldi, who, ten minutes ago, was my neighbor offering to give me dating advice, becomes my live-in fake boyfriend for the next week.

I really need to work on my impulse control.

eleven

. . .

Brandon

I UNLOCK my apartment door and step aside to let Stella pass, watching her as she paces a tight circle in my entryway like a caged animal.

"Fuck, fuck, fuckity, fuck," she mutters, wrapping her arms around herself. "I just told my mother you're my boyfriend. My mother, Brandon."

"Stella—"

"She's going to expect us to act like a couple. Like, a real couple." She stops pacing and stares at me with wide, panicked eyes. "What have I done?"

The sight of normally composed, always-has-a-plan Stella completely losing her shit is, honestly, kind of endearing. I should be pissed. Any sane person would be pissed about being volunteered as someone's fake boyfriend without so much as a heads up.

But instead, I find myself wanting to laugh.

"She loves hotels. She's up to something. I think she's

forcing us together because I said it was new and early and she's trying to make sure it turns into something!"

"Breathe," I tell her, closing the door behind us. "It's not the end of the world."

"Not the end of the—" She gapes at me. "Brandon, I just dragged you into the most ridiculous fake dating scheme in the history of fake dating schemes. You should be furious. You should be throwing me out of your apartment. You should be—"

"Making you some tea and figuring out how to pull this off without your mom realizing you're a terrible liar?"

She blinks. "You're not mad?"

I should be. I really should be. But the truth is, watching Stella panic is actually making me feel weirdly protective. Plus, there's something about the way she looked when she asked for my help with the whole flirting-with-guys thing earlier—although it still irritates me that she thinks landing a decent guy is some kind of impossible mission she needs my expertise to complete.

"Look, you were cornered. Your mom ambushed you." I head to the kitchen, mostly because I need something to do with my hands. "Besides, didn't you just ask me to help you get better at talking to guys? Consider this an intensive workshop."

"An intensive workshop," she repeats slowly.

"Sure. Think of it like stunt work. It's all about selling the illusion, right? Making something fake look completely real." I ditch the tea and grab two beers from the fridge instead because this conversation definitely requires alcohol. "I've taught actors how to throw convincing punches and fall down stairs without actually getting hurt. How hard can it be to teach someone to fake a relationship?"

She grabs the beer I offer her and immediately takes a long gulp. "You make it sound so simple."

"Because it is simple. We just need to establish some ground rules so neither of us accidentally makes this weird."

"Ground rules. Yes. I love ground rules." She perches on my coffee table, facing me with the intensity of someone about to negotiate a million-dollar deal. "What kind of ground rules?"

"First, we're clear that this is purely business, right? We're friends helping each other out. Nothing more." I take a sip of my beer, keeping my voice casual. "No catching feelings, no blurred lines. When this is over, we go back to exactly how things were before."

"Absolutely," she says quickly. "This is just temporary. A favor between friends."

"Good. Second question. Exactly how much acting are we talking about here? How often do you think we'll be around your mom together?"

"Not that much, honestly. I have work, and you're on set most of the time anyway." She nods, and I can see her confidence growing. "Maybe a meal or two with her. It's not like we'll be performing twenty-four-seven."

I nod. "Okay, so when we are with your mom, what kind of touching is acceptable? Hand holding? Sitting close together?"

"Basic couple stuff. Nothing dramatic." She waves her hand like she's shooing away my concerns. "Maybe you put your arm around me like you did tonight. We sit close together. Act like we actually like each other."

"I do actually like you."

"You know what I mean." Her cheeks flush slightly. "Like we like each other in a couple way."

"And what about kissing?"

The question just hangs there between us, and I watch her face cycle through about six different expressions before settling on determined.

"If the situation absolutely requires it," she says finally. "But my mom's not going to expect us to make out in front of her. She's Southern."

"But if she does expect it?"

"Then yes. If the situation absolutely requires it." She meets my eyes directly. "Would that be okay?"

Any guy in his right mind would say yes to kissing Stella Rhodes, fake relationship or not. She's gorgeous, obviously, but it's more than that. She's... I don't know. Easy to be around. Comfortable. The kind of person who makes you feel like you're the funniest, most interesting version of yourself, and all she's doing is paying attention to you.

Which is probably why I'm not nearly as bothered by this whole fake boyfriend thing as I should be.

"Yeah," I say, trying to sound casual about it. "That's fine. Totally professional."

"Professional," she agrees, though something in her voice makes me think she's trying to convince herself as much as me.

"And we're both clear that whatever happens during this

whole thing, it doesn't change our friendship. We don't let it get complicated."

"Right. No complications. We're just two friends doing each other a favor."

"Exactly." I raise my beer. "To keeping it simple."

"To keeping it simple," she echoes, clinking her bottle against mine.

"You can take my bedroom," I continue, standing up. "I'll sleep on the couch."

"Brandon, no. This is your apartment. I can't kick you out of your own bed."

"You're not kicking me out. I'm offering." I head toward my bedroom to grab some pillows and blankets. "Besides, your mom would expect me to be a gentleman about sleeping arrangements."

"Are you sure?"

"Positive. Make yourself at home."

I gather what I need for the couch and return to find Stella standing in my living room, looking uncertain again. "I didn't grab a nightgown. Or a toothbrush. Or—"

"Check the bathroom. I keep extra toothbrushes for when my sisters visit. And you can borrow one of my t-shirts to sleep in."

"Thanks." She gives me a soft smile that does weird things to my chest. "Really, Brandon. Thank you for this."

"Don't mention it."

I watch her disappear into my bedroom, and a few minutes later, I hear the shower turn on. The sound of running water shouldn't affect me, but knowing that Stella is naked less than twenty feet away makes my brain go to places it definitely shouldn't.

I try to focus on setting up my makeshift bed on the couch, fluffing pillows and arranging blankets with more attention than the task requires. But I can't stop thinking about her in my shower, using my soap, standing under the hot spray with water running down her naked body.

This is completely inappropriate. She's my friend. She's here because she trusts me to help her, not because she wants anything to happen between us. The fact that my dick is getting hard is just basic biology. Any man would have the same reaction to an attractive woman in such close proximity.

It doesn't mean anything.

A few minutes later, the sound of her moving around my bedroom filters through the wall. The soft pad of her bare feet across my hardwood floors. The rustle of fabric as she changes into whatever shirt she borrowed from my dresser.

I close my eyes and take a deep breath, willing my body to calm down. This is about helping her achieve a goal, nothing more. I'll teach her what she wants to know about confidence and appeal, she'll get Mason or some other guy, and we'll all move on with our lives.

Simple. Clean. Professional.

So, why does the thought of teaching Stella how to be irresistible make my stomach twist into knots?

I lie on my couch, staring up at the ceiling and listening to the sounds of her settling into my bed. The rustle of sheets, the soft sigh as she gets comfortable, the gradual quiet that means she's falling asleep.

This is going to be a very long few days.

twelve

. . .

Stella

GIRL GANG GROUP CHAT

STELLA

SOS. Operation Plus-One has officially become Operation Fake Boyfriend. My mother showed up unannounced last night and I panicked and told her Brandon is my boyfriend. FML.

JESS

Wait WHAT? Brandon? Like our friend Brandon? Your neighbor Brandon?

NATALIE

OMG YES. I can totally see you two together! Maybe this will actually go somewhere 👀

STELLA

Nat, NO. This is a disaster management situation, not a matchmaking opportunity.

SOPHIA

Honestly? This is best case scenario. Brandon's a great guy and an even better friend. Why didn't we think of this in the first place? He's perfect to stall your mom and buy you time.

BLAIR

I'm sorry, can we back up to the part where your mother just SHOWED UP? Without warning? That woman needs to learn about boundaries. And maybe the concept of calling first.

JESS

Stella, be careful. This feels very familiar and I've seen how these things can get... complicated. Don't get sucked in and mistake the fake feelings for something else.

NATALIE

Or DO get sucked in because Brandon is hot and you're both single and life is short

BLAIR

Natalie, you're not helping.

STELLA

We're just friends, and he's just helping me out. It's only for a few days. What could go wrong?

SOPHIA

Famous last words...

JESS

Literally never ask that question. It's like asking the universe to intervene.

NATALIE

Keep us posted! I want details. ALL the details.

BLAIR

Gotta run, baby time, but Stella, you're a grown woman with your own life. Just remember you are the one in charge!

STELLA

Thanks guys. Wish me luck.

SOPHIA

You've got this. And Brandon's got your back.

JESS

Just…be careful. Fake dating can get messy fast.

NATALIE

Or don't be careful at all! Sometimes messy can be fun

thirteen

. . .

Stella

"SO, WHEN DID WE START DATING?" Brandon asks, adjusting his collar in the mirror by his front door. He's wearing dark jeans and a maroon button-down shirt that brings out his eyes, and I'm trying very hard not to notice how good he looks when he's dressed for a night out.

"Let's keep it as close to the truth as possible," I say, smoothing down my light blue wrap dress for the third time. "We started hanging out when I moved in across the hall, and then one thing led to another."

"One thing led to another," he repeats, grinning. "Very romantic."

"It doesn't have to be romantic. It just has to be believable." I grab my purse and check my reflection one more time. "Ready to go convince my mother we're madly in love?"

"Are we madly in love? Because that seems like important information for the fake boyfriend to have."

I pause at his front door. "Good question. How in love should we be at this point?"

"I don't know. You're the one who created this situation." He steps closer, and suddenly, the space between us feels charged. "But if we're going to sell this, we should probably figure it out."

"Right." I can smell his cologne, something clean and masculine that makes me want to lean closer. "We're...smitten, head over heels, but not so crazy about each other that it would be devastating if things didn't work out."

Something flickers across his face so quickly that I almost miss it. "Right. Can't make it too dramatic for when we eventually..." He trails off, his jaw tightening slightly.

"Break up," I finish, and the words feel heavier than they should. "Exactly. We're in that honeymoon phase where everything feels new and exciting but still realistic enough that if we decide we're better as friends, it won't seem weird."

"The honeymoon phase," he says softly, his eyes dropping to my lips for just a moment. "Got it."

The entry suddenly feels too small, too warm. I clear my throat and reach for the door handle. "We should get my mother."

We cross the hall to my apartment, where I find my mother already waiting with her purse and a fresh coat of lipstick. She takes one look at us standing together and practically beams.

"Don't you two look lovely," she says, kissing my cheek carefully to avoid smudging her makeup. "Brandon, that shirt brings out your eyes beautifully."

"Thank you, Mrs. Rhodes. You look stunning as always."

She actually giggles. My fifty-two-year-old mother giggles

like a teenager, and I realize Brandon's charm is going to be a much bigger problem than I anticipated.

The restaurant I chose is exactly the kind of place my mother loves, with white tablecloths, soft lighting, and a wine list with multiple pages. It's upscale enough to impress her but not so fancy that we'll feel out of place. Brandon holds doors, pulls out chairs, and orders wine with the confidence of someone who's done this a thousand times.

"So, tell me," my mother says once we're settled, "how exactly did you two go from neighbors to something more?"

I stiffen at the question, but Brandon jumps in smoothly. "It was gradual, really. Stella's one of those people who just draws you in without trying. Smart, funny, completely oblivious to how amazing she is." He takes my hand, and his thumb brushes across my knuckles. "I was a goner pretty quickly."

The casual way he touches me, like it's the most natural thing in the world, sends a zing through my stomach. His hand is warm and callused from stunt work, and when he strokes his thumb across my skin, I have to remind myself this is all an act.

"That's so sweet," my mother coos. "And Stella, what drew you to Brandon?"

"He's..." I look at him, at the way he's watching me with those warm brown eyes, and for a moment, I forget I'm supposed to be acting. "He's genuinely kind. Not performatively nice like a lot of people in this town, but actually good. He drops everything to help a friend, remembers the little things that matter to you, and he's never once made me feel like I need to be someone else around him."

I pause, surprised by how easily the words are coming. "And he's fearless in this quiet way. He throws himself off buildings for a living, but it's more than that. He's not afraid to be himself, to take up space, to care about people openly. He makes loyalty look effortless."

Something shifts in Brandon's expression, like he's hearing these words for the first time. Which, I realize, he is.

"Plus," I add, trying to lighten the suddenly heavy moment, "he makes me laugh until my stomach hurts, and he's the only person I know who takes reality TV as seriously as I do. And he's not hard to look at."

When the waiter approaches, Brandon glances between both our menus. "The salmon's caught locally," he says quietly, leaning closer and pointing to the listing on my menu. "And they do that lemon herb thing you like."

"Perfect," I say, closing my menu with a smile. "I assume you're getting the ribeye, medium rare, no sides because you're going to eat half my vegetables anyway?"

"You know me too well," he says with a grin.

When the bread arrives, he automatically pushes the basket closer to me, knowing I always go for the warm rolls first.

"Tell me about your charity work," Brandon says to my mother, and as she launches into a detailed explanation of the children's hospital fundraiser she's organizing, his hand comes to rest casually on the back of my chair, and his thumb traces lazy circles on my shoulder blade. The touch is so light I'm not even sure he realizes he's doing it, but it's making it very difficult to concentrate on the conversation.

"Brandon, you simply must come to the fundraising gala

with Stella next month," my mother says as our entrées arrive. "It's always such a lovely event, and I know she'd love to have you there as her date."

I freeze with my fork halfway to my mouth. "Mama, we haven't even talked about—"

"Of course I'd love to be there," Brandon says smoothly as his knee presses against mine under the table. "If Stella wants me there."

"Of course she does," my mother says with a knowing smile. "And Brandon, when you come home with Stella for Christmas—well, if you come home with her—you'll have to try my famous bourbon pecan pie."

"When he comes home for Christmas?" I repeat, my voice pitched slightly higher than normal.

"If," my mother corrects, though her tone suggests she's already planning the menu. "I'm just saying Brandon seems like the kind of man who'd fit right in with our family traditions."

Brandon's hand finds mine on the table, and he tangles our fingers together. "I'd be honored to be included in any family traditions," he says, and the sincerity in his voice makes my chest tight. What is he doing? There's no way I'll be ready to bring a boyfriend home for Christmas.

"Stella!" A familiar voice pulls me away from the conversation, and when I look up, I see Ava St. James approaching our table, elegant as always in a black pantsuit.

"Ava, hi!" I stand to give her a quick hug, my mind racing. "What a lovely surprise."

Her eyes drift curiously to our table, and I realize she's waiting for an introduction.

"Ava, I'd like you to meet my mother, Caroline Rhodes, and this is Brandon Grimaldi." I pause, then realize I forgot the most important part. "My boyfriend."

Yeah, there, that wasn't awkward at all.

Brandon stands and extends his hand with that devastating smile. "Ms. St. James, it's a pleasure to meet you."

"Oh, my goodness," my mother breathes, clearly starstruck. "I'm such a fan of your work. I think I've seen every movie you've starred in."

"You're very kind," Ava says graciously, shaking hands with both of them. "I hope you're enjoying your evening."

"We are, thank you," Brandon says smoothly at the same time my mother says, "Very much so!"

"Wonderful. Well, I don't want to interrupt your dinner," Ava replies with a warm smile. "I'll see you at Helena's premiere next week?"

"Yes, we'll all be there," I say, feeling a little punchy that if Brandon feels good enough to invite himself to Christmas, he should be fine to attend a premiere with me next week.

After she leaves, I settle back in my chair. Something about the encounter makes me fidget with my napkin.

Brandon leans into me, and his hand covers mine. "Everything okay?"

"Fine," I say, though I'm not entirely sure why the introduction made me feel so exposed. "Just mixing professional and personal, you know?"

His fingers squeeze mine gently, warm and reassuring. "I'm sure there's nothing to worry about."

On our way out of the restaurant, my mother stops to use the restroom, leaving Brandon and me alone by the coat check. He's standing close enough that I can see the flecks of gold in his brown eyes, can smell that cologne that's been driving me crazy all evening.

"You're really good at this," I say quietly.

"Good at what?"

"The boyfriend thing. The touching, the sweet comments, making my mother fall in love with you." I look up at him. "I almost believe it myself."

"Stella, I—" He stops mid-sentence, his eyes focused on something over my shoulder. "Shit."

"What?"

Before I can turn around, his hand cups my jaw, and he's kissing me. Not a sweet, performative kiss for my mother's benefit, but something deeper, more urgent. His other arm wraps around my waist, pulling me flush with his body as his mouth moves against mine.

Holy shit, I'm kissing Brandon. Brandon is kissing me. And, oh, my God, he's incredible at this. No wonder half the women in LA have his number saved in their phones. This is not the casual peck I was expecting.

I'm so surprised I don't react at first, but then my hands find his chest, and I'm kissing him back, completely lost in the heat of his mouth. My fingers curl into his shirt as I lean into his lips shamelessly.

When we break apart, I'm breathless and slightly dazed, trying to remember how to form coherent thoughts. "What was that for?"

"Director from a project I turned down last month," he says quietly, glancing over my shoulder. "Guy's been harassing me about it ever since, and he just spotted us. He was heading over here, but he won't interrupt what looks like an intimate moment with my girlfriend. Coast is clear now."

Before I can process this information, my mother reappears, looking satisfied and ready to go.

"Well!" she says, fanning herself dramatically. "What'd I miss?"

"Just telling Stella how beautiful she looks tonight," Brandon says smoothly, though I notice his voice is slightly rough around the edges.

"You two are just precious," my mother coos, pulling out her phone. "I absolutely must get a picture. You look so perfect together."

I'm still processing what just happened, the urgency of that kiss and the way my entire body responded to it, so I barely register Brandon pulling me against his side for the photo. His hand settles on my hip, and when his fingers tighten slightly, I'm reminded of how solid and warm he felt pressed against me just moments ago.

"Beautiful," my mother says, snapping several photos. "Oh, this one's perfect."

She shows us the image, and through my daze, I can see that we do look good together. Natural. Like we actually belong in each other's arms.

"We should probably get you home, Mrs. Rhodes," Brandon says, his voice carefully controlled. "It's getting late."

But as we walk to his car, I catch him glancing at me when he thinks I'm not looking, and I wonder if he's feeling the same confusion I am. Because that kiss felt like a lot of things, but acting wasn't one of them.

fourteen

. . .

Brandon

"THANK you for such a wonderful evening, Brandon," Caroline says, pulling me into one of her signature hugs.

"Thank you for dinner, Mrs. Rhodes. It was my pleasure."

"Please, call me Caroline. We're practically family now." She beams at me, then glances at Stella. "You two have a good night. Don't keep her up too late."

The implication in her voice makes my face warm, but I just smile and nod. "Of course. Goodnight, Caroline."

As soon as her door closes, Stella and I are alone in the hallway. The space between us crackles with unspoken tension. She's still not quite meeting my eyes, and she's fidgeting with her purse strap.

"Well," she says brightly, her voice pitched slightly higher than normal. "That went well, I think."

"Really well," I agree, unlocking my apartment door. "Your mom seems happy."

"She loves you. I think she's already planning our

wedding." She laughs, but it sounds forced. "Which is ridiculous, obviously."

"Obviously."

We step into my apartment, and suddenly, the space feels too small, too intimate. The memory of that kiss hangs between us like a live wire, and I can see from the way Stella is carefully not looking at me that she's thinking about it, too.

We're both talking too fast, being too polite, working too hard to pretend that nothing earth-shattering happened outside the restaurant.

"Thanks again for tonight," she says, pausing near the hallway. "You were really great. Very convincing."

"So were you."

It was just acting, I remind myself. We were selling a performance for her mother. The fact that my heart is still racing and I can still taste her on my lips doesn't mean anything. It can't mean anything.

She nods once, then shifts awkwardly. "I'm going to get ready for bed. Thanks again for letting me take the bed."

"Actually, do you mind if I grab a quick shower first? Won't take long."

"Of course. Take your time. I'm just going to read for a bit."

She heads toward my bedroom, and I stand in my living room for a moment, running a hand through my hair and trying to process everything. That kiss felt real, but it wasn't. She's a better actress than I gave her credit for. The way she responded was just her selling the performance. I need to remember that this is all pretend and get my head back in the game.

I head for the bathroom, where I turn the shower on as hot as it will go.

The water feels good against my shoulders. I lean against the shower wall, letting the steam build around me, and try not to think of Stella's lips while I'm naked in here.

This is fake. All of it. The hand holding, the casual touches, the way I keep finding excuses to brush her hair back or rest my palm on her lower back. But being there with her in that restaurant, sitting across from her mother, nothing about it felt fake.

When Caroline started talking about Christmas and the upcoming charity gala, asking if I'd be there like it was a given, I should have felt trapped, should have been looking for ways to deflect or keep things vague. Instead, I found myself meaning it when I said I'd be honored to be included. The thought of spending holidays with Stella, of being the person she brings home to meet her family, doesn't make me want to run.

Which is insane. This is Stella. My neighbor. My friend. The woman who asks me to kill spiders in her apartment and steals spring rolls from my takeout containers.

But tonight, in that blue dress that showed off her legs and made her eyes look like the ocean, she was something else entirely. She was stunning. Confident. The kind of woman who could walk into any room and own it without even trying. And when her mother was going on about how perfect we looked together, all I could think was that maybe she was right.

My hand moves to my cock almost without conscious thought, already half-hard from remembering the way Stella felt pressed against me during that kiss. Because Christ, that kiss. What started as a way to avoid an awkward conversation with a director I never want to work with again turned into something that nearly made me forget we were in a public place.

The way she responded, the little sound she made when my tongue touched hers, the way her hands fisted in my shirt like she couldn't get close enough. For those few seconds, there was nothing fake about what was happening between us. Just pure want.

I stroke myself slowly, remembering the taste of her, the way she melted against me like she'd been waiting for that kiss as much as I had. My other hand braces against the shower wall as I pick up the pace, and I let the hot water run over my shoulders while I think about what it would be like to kiss her again. To take my time with it instead of having to pull away.

I shouldn't be doing this. Shouldn't be getting off to thoughts of Stella while she's sleeping in my bed just behind the bathroom door. But the image of her curled up in my sheets, all soft and warm and trusting enough to let her guard down in my space, only makes me harder.

I think about her in those little shorts she sleeps in, the ones that show off her legs and ride up when she stretches. About the thin tank tops she wears that leave nothing to the imagination. About what it would be like to slip into bed beside her, to wake up with her hair spread across my pillow and her body pressed against mine.

The thought pushes me over the edge, and I come with a strangled groan that I hope to hell the shower noise covers. I lean against the wall for a moment, breathing hard and trying to process what this means. Jerking off to thoughts of my fake girlfriend, my neighbor, my friend, while she sleeps in my bed probably crosses some kind of line in the friendship universe.

I finish washing up and turn off the water before grabbing a towel and wrapping it around my waist. When I open the bathroom door, the apartment is quiet except for the soft sound of Stella's breathing from my bedroom. I grab a pair of boxers from my dresser, trying to be as quiet as possible, and glance at the bed.

She's curled up on her side, facing away from me, with the book she was reading on the bed beside her and the lamp on my nightstand still glowing. She looks so peaceful, so perfectly right in my space, that something shifts in my chest.

I gently pull the covers over her, flip off the light, and slip out of the bedroom as quietly as I can. Then I settle onto the couch with a blanket and a pillow. But as I lie there in the dark, thinking about her sleeping in my bed, I can't shake the feeling that something shifted between us tonight.

Which is exactly why I need to get this back on track. Back to what we agreed on. I'm supposed to be helping her learn how to talk to guys, how to project confidence, how to get the attention she wants from someone who could actually give her what she's looking for. Not getting distracted by fake relationship performances that feel way too real.

I'll bring her to a wrap party tomorrow night. It'll be perfect. Lots of single guys, casual atmosphere, and a good opportunity for her to practice everything we've been working on. Maybe I'll give her an assignment, something concrete to focus on, like asking someone for their number, or better yet, asking someone out on a date.

I just need to remember that I'm the teacher here, not a participant. Good teachers want their students to succeed, and success means finding a guy who can be her real boyfriend.

fifteen

. . .

Stella

"HONEY, I'M HOME!" I call out as I push through Brandon's door before dropping my keys on his console table. After eight hours of following my mother through every boutique in Beverly Hills, I'm exhausted, and my feet are killing me, but at least she found the perfect dress for the charity gala. Brandon and I have managed to act normal around each other since the kiss, but I'd be lying if I said I didn't think about it more than I should.

"Perfect timing." Brandon appears from his bedroom, and I have to do a double take. Gone are his usual jeans and t-shirt. Instead, he's wearing dark slacks and a white button-down that makes his shoulders look impossibly broad. His sleeves are rolled up, and yep, his forearms are perfection.

"You're staring, sunshine." He smirks as he brushes by me, headed for the kitchen.

I blink at him, confused. "Where are you going?"

"We," he says, grabbing his keys and wallet from the kitchen counter, "are going to a party in the Hills. Wrap party for that new thriller where I doubled in the snow ski scene. You're my plus-one, and I'm going to be your wingman."

My stomach drops. "Brandon, no. I'm not ready for—"

"Tonight," he continues, completely ignoring my panic, "you're going to ask a guy out on a date."

I let out an honest-to-God squeal. "No way! You're out of your mind. I can't just walk up to some random guy and—"

"Fine, then your goal will be to get a guy's phone number." He moves toward me with that easy confidence. "And I have to go. My agent friend has been bugging me about showing up to these things." He raises his eyebrow to match it perfectly with his glare. It's me. I'm the agent friend that's been bugging him.

"Besides, I don't want to go alone. And this will be the perfect place for you to practice."

"Practice for what, exactly? Public humiliation?"

He grins, and there's something wicked in it. "Practice for dealing with the worst Hollywood has to offer. These people are so self-absorbed they think a compliment about their shoes is worthy of a standing ovation. They're like emotional vampires who feed on flattery and name dropping."

Despite my terror, I snort with laughter. "That's horrible."

"But accurate. Come on, Stella. You could meet the love of your life tonight, or at least get enough practice so you don't feel awkward around Mason next time you see him."

The mention of Mason makes my resolve stronger. Brandon's right. If I'm really determined to get a boyfriend, I need to be the kind of confident woman who doesn't blend into the background.

"Fine," I say. "Give me a minute to change."

Thirty minutes later, we're winding up into the Hollywood Hills in Brandon's car, and my palms are sweating. The house, when we finally reach it, is one of those sprawling modern monstrosities that looks like it's carved into the mountainside. Floor-to-ceiling windows reveal glimpses of beautiful people holding expensive drinks.

"Holy shit," I breathe.

"Language, sunshine," Brandon teases, but his hand finds the small of my back as we walk to the front door. "You've been to parties before."

"Not like this." And it's true. Sure, I've been to industry events with Blair, but this feels different. More exclusive. More intimidating.

The door opens before we can knock, and we're swept into a world of marble floors and dramatic lighting. The back wall is entirely glass, showcasing a view that stretches from downtown to the ocean, with the city spread out below us like a glittering carpet. Fresh white orchids the size of my head sit on every surface, and the furniture looks like it belongs in an architectural magazine.

"Try not to look so impressed," Brandon murmurs in my ear, his breath warm against my skin. "These people can smell an outsider from a mile away."

But I can't help it. Even after almost six years in LA, even after all the fancy restaurants and premieres I've attended with clients, this still takes my breath away.

"Brandon! You actually showed up!" A tall brunette in

a dress that highlights every perfect curve of her body glides over to us. She air-kisses Brandon's cheeks like they're old friends, and I can't help but stare, feeling a subtle twist of envy in my gut. Her confidence is impressive.

"Couldn't miss seeing you," he says smoothly. "Vera, this is Stella. Stella, Vera's our producer."

Vera's smile is polite but dismissive as she looks me over. "Nice to meet you. Are you an actress?"

"Agent," I say, trying to inject some confidence into my voice. "I work with Blair Bennett."

That gets her attention. "Blair Bennett? She's brilliant. Absolutely ruthless, but brilliant."

Before I have a chance to respond, Vera's attention is already moving to the next guest, dismissing us with the kind of polite finality that makes it clear our conversation is over. I'm about to suggest that we find the bar when something catches my eye across the room—a flash of dark hair with purple streaks that I'd recognize anywhere.

"Is that..." I squint through the crowd. "Oh, my God."

"Is that who?"

"Let's go." I practically drag Brandon across the room. "Natalie! What are you doing here?"

I can't hide my excitement as I spot my yoga friend near the bar, looking surprisingly at home among the Hollywood elite. She turns, and her face lights up when she sees me.

"Stella! What a surprise!" She's wearing a flowing maxi dress that somehow manages to look both bohemian and elegant, and her dark hair falls in loose waves.

"I had no idea you moved in these circles."

Natalie's cheeks flush slightly. "I'm just...networking. Learning about the business side of things."

Before I can question her further, a familiar voice interrupts.

"Well, well. Look what the cat dragged in."

I turn to find Jake approaching with two drinks in hand, looking much more put-together than he did at Sophia and Grant's wedding. His hair is actually styled, and he's traded the dark circles under his eyes for a bright smile.

"Jake!" I hug him quickly. "I didn't know you'd be here, either. Do you know Natalie? Natalie, this is Jake. He works with Wyatt and organizes the ever-famous Manmorial Weekend."

Jake extends his hand to Natalie, and there's a beat where they just look at each other, with some kind of electric recognition passing between them that makes me feel like I'm interrupting something. "Nice to meet you, Natalie."

"Likewise." She takes his hand, and I swear there's a little spark when they touch.

"I didn't see my invitation for this year's event," Brandon interjects with mock offense.

Jake grins. "Hey, if you could find a woman and settle down, you'd get an invitation. That's what Manmorial is all about—attached men getting away for some bonding time."

"Maybe the rules change this year?" Brandon asks, and there's something careful in his tone.

Jake's expression flickers. "Touché. I guess you are right. I am single now."

"Oh," Natalie says, her voice softening. "I'm sorry. Breakups suck."

Jake shrugs, trying to play it off. "Yeah, well, these things happen."

"But hey," Natalie continues with a mischievous glint in her eye, "that means Brandon would be eligible for Manmorial this year, right? Since he and Stella are dating now." She shoots me a quick wink that makes my stomach drop.

Jake's eyebrows shoot up as he looks between Brandon and me. "What? You two are dating?" His gaze settles on Brandon with newfound interest. "When did this happen? How did I miss this?"

Brandon clears his throat, and his hand finds my lower back. "You didn't miss anything. We're not actually dating."

"My mom's visiting," I say quickly, lowering my voice. "And I may have told her I had a boyfriend to get her off my back about setting me up. Brandon's helping me out by playing the part until she leaves."

"Ah." Jake nods with understanding. "The fake boyfriend situation. Classic."

"They make a cute couple, though, right?" Natalie says with a grin, looking between us. "I mean, you two do have great chemistry."

Jake studies us with amusement. "You know what? She's not wrong. You two actually seem pretty natural together. No way this could turn into something real?"

"No," Brandon and I say simultaneously, maybe a little too quickly.

"Come on, let's get a drink, and we can talk more about Manmorial weekend."

Before Brandon can protest, Jake is already steering him

toward the bar, leaving me alone with Natalie, who's trying very hard not to look smug.

"What was that?" I hiss.

"What? I'm just helping maintain your cover story," she says innocently. "Besides, I thought you'd want people to know you're dating Brandon. Isn't that the whole point?"

"No, it's not the whole point. We're only doing this for my mother's benefit." I watch as Jake gestures animatedly while talking to Brandon.

"You're enjoying this way too much," I mutter.

Natalie grins. "Maybe a little."

We slip right back into our usual rhythm of trading updates, dissecting who's here with whom, and whispering commentary that would absolutely get us blacklisted if anyone overheard. While Natalie waits on the bartender to mix her another drink, I glance across the room and spot Brandon talking to a group of women—actresses, by the look of them—and they're hanging on his every word.

"You okay?" Natalie asks, waving a hand in front of my face.

"Fine," I say quickly, snapping my eyes away from the love fest. "I was just observing."

"Observing Brandon work his magic?" Natalie asks with a slight smile.

"He's supposed to be teaching me how to be more confident with men."

Natalie snorts. "That's not confidence. That's a master class in seduction. The man's got game."

As if to prove Natalie's point, Brandon brushes a strand of hair away from the blonde's face while listening intently to whatever she's saying. The gesture is so smooth and natural that she melts into it, and I can see the other women watching, waiting for their turn to have his attention.

"This is ridiculous," I mutter, more to myself than to Natalie.

"What is?" Natalie asks.

I gesture toward Brandon and his fan club. "This whole confidence lesson thing. Look at them." A blonde in a red dress tosses her hair back as she laughs at something he said, leaning in closer with each exchange. Another woman touches his arm while making a point, completely at ease in her own skin. "They just walk up and start conversations like it's nothing. They're flirty and natural and completely comfortable. Meanwhile, I freeze up every time I see Mason in the hallway."

"Maybe you're overthinking it," Natalie suggests. "What if you just talked to Mason the way you talk to everyone else?"

"But that's the problem!" I say, my frustration building. "I can't just be Stella around guys I'm attracted to. Stella is boring. Stella blends into the wallpaper. Stella needs to learn how to be..." I wave my hand toward the group of gorgeous women surrounding Brandon. "Like that."

Before Natalie can respond, I spot a tall guy with sandy brown hair and an easy smile standing by the bar. He's attractive in that clean-cut, approachable way and definitely someone I can practice on without feeling completely intimidated.

I decide it's time to put Brandon's lessons into action. "Be right back," I tell Natalie.

I take a deep breath and channel every confident woman I've ever seen in a movie. "Hi there," I say, walking up to the unsuspecting guy. "I'm Stella. Great party, right?"

He looks genuinely pleased by the approach, though something flickers across his face that I can't quite read. "David," he replies. "It really is. Are you part of the production?"

"No, I'm here with friends. I'm a talent agent." So far, so good. I remember Brandon saying confident women use their environment, so I casually lean back against the bar like I've seen actresses do in films. Except my elbow slides right off the edge, sending my entire body lurching sideways into the person next to me.

"Oh, my God, I'm so sorry!" I grab wildly to steady their martini, which sloshes dangerously but doesn't spill. The woman gives me a look that could freeze lava.

"Are you...okay?" David asks. His eyebrows have climbed toward his hairline.

"Totally fine! Just, you know, gravity." I laugh too loudly. "What about you? Do you work in the industry?"

"Film editor. I worked on this one, actually." He gestures at the party around us, taking a small step back. "It's always surreal seeing the final product after spending months in the editing bay."

"That must be so satisfying, though, seeing everything come together." Brandon said eye contact was key, so I lock my gaze onto David's face with laser focus. I'm going to nail this part.

After about ten seconds of my unblinking stare, David

reaches up and touches his cheek. "Do I have something on my face?"

"No! No, you're perfect. I mean, your face is fine. Clean." Oh, God. "I was just listening. You're very interesting."

He looks uncertain. "O-kay. Well, I was saying there's something magical about finding the perfect cut that makes a scene come alive."

I catch movement in my peripheral vision. Brandon's across the patio with Jake, and when he notices me talking to David, he gives me what I think is an encouraging nod. This gives me the confidence boost I need to try his casual touching technique.

I reach out to touch David's arm while he's talking, but my timing is spectacularly off. He's mid-gesture, bringing his drink to his lips, and my hand collides with his elbow just as the glass reaches his mouth.

Beer splashes across his chin and down his shirt.

"Oh no, oh no, oh no!" I grab napkins from the bar, frantically dabbing at his shirt while he stands there in shock. "I'm so sorry! I don't know why I did that!"

"It's okay," he says, gently taking the napkins from me before I can cause more damage. "Really."

But I can see in his eyes that he's starting to wonder if I'm having some kind of medical episode.

"You know what?" I say, my voice somehow choosing this moment to drop into what I think is a sultry register but sounds more like I've been chain smoking for twenty years. "I'd love to hear more about it. Would you maybe want to get coffee sometime this week?"

David freezes, a napkin halfway to his damp shirt, staring at me like he's trying to solve a puzzle. "Oh, um."

The silence stretches just long enough for panic to set in.

"Or dinner!" I blurt out. "Or lunch! Or really any meal. I'm very flexible about meals. Very accommodating. Food-wise."

"That's really nice of you," he says carefully, taking a small step back, "but I'm actually seeing someone."

The rejection hits me like a physical blow, made worse by the fact that I can't blame him. If someone had stared at me like a serial killer, physically assaulted me mid-sip, and then propositioned me in a voice that belonged in a sex tape, I'd probably claim to be seeing someone, too.

"Oh! Of course you are. You seem like someone who would be seeing someone. Very dateable. Obviously."

He nods slowly, like he's trying not to make any sudden movements. "Thanks? I should probably get back to my friends."

"Absolutely! Great talking to you, David!"

He walks away quickly, and I notice him glance back once, like he's making sure I'm not following him.

I stand there for a moment, contemplating whether it's possible to die of mortification, then trudge back to Natalie.

"Well," she says, clearly having witnessed the entire cata-strophe, "that was educational."

"Don't."

"I'm just saying, I've never seen someone weaponize flirting before."

I bury my face in my hands. "Brandon is going to have so much material to work with."

sixteen

. . .

Brandon

I'M STANDING at my kitchen counter, staring into my coffee mug like it will either solve all my problems or give me a glimpse into the future. The caffeine isn't doing much to clear the fog of confusion that's been sitting in my chest since last night.

Stella didn't get a date. In fact, she spectacularly crashed and burned with that editor guy in what might have been the most entertaining train wreck I've witnessed in years. I should feel bad for her because she was mortified and, as her friend and self-appointed confidence coach, her failure reflects poorly on my teaching abilities.

So, why do I feel relieved?

I take another sip of coffee and try to rationalize it. Maybe I'm just protective of her. Maybe my instincts knew that the guy wasn't right for her. But even as I'm running through perfectly reasonable explanations, I know they're bullshit. The truth is, watching her attempt to flirt with someone else made me want to march over there and remind everyone in that room that she was there with me.

Which is insane because I'm supposed to be helping her succeed with other guys. But the relief I felt when he walked away wasn't the reaction of a good friend or a supportive teacher.

It was the reaction of a guy who didn't want to watch the woman he—

No. Not going there.

The sound of bare feet on hardwood pulls me from my spiral, and I look up to see Stella padding into the kitchen wearing one of my t-shirts and those tiny sleep shorts that have been driving me crazy for the past few days. Her hair is messy from sleep, and she looks soft and rumpled—and so gorgeous it actually hurts.

"Morning," she says, heading straight for the coffee pot with the single-minded determination of someone who doesn't function without caffeine.

"Morning. Sleep well?"

"Really well, actually." She pours her coffee and leans against the counter across from me, and there's something different about her posture. More confident, maybe. Like last night's success gave her a boost.

"Are we meeting your mom today? Any boyfriend duties I need to prepare for?"

A light chuckle escapes as she brings the mug to her lips for a sip. "Nope, you're off the hook. We're doing a spa day, so we'll be there all afternoon."

"That sounds relaxing."

"We'll see. I'm sure there will be plenty of questions

about you, so while you won't be there in person, your name will definitely come up."

"I'm flattered to be spa conversation material."

Her eyes crinkle with amusement over the rim of her mug. "Don't let it go to your head." The smile fades into something more thoughtful. "But I've been thinking about what you said. About confidence being something you practice until it becomes real."

"Yeah?"

"Well, watching you last night, seeing how easy it is for you to talk to people, especially those women who kept gravitating toward you." She pauses, taking a sip of her coffee. "It made me realize that maybe some of my insecurities aren't just about confidence. Maybe they're about experience."

I feel my stomach tighten. "What kind of experience?"

"That's what I want to talk to you about." She sets down her mug and reaches for a notebook on the counter. "I made a list of things I'm curious about. Things I'd like your help with, if you're willing."

She hands me the handwritten list, and I stare at it. Her careful cursive loops across the page look like something out of a finishing school manual, which makes the content even more jarring.

Stella's Confidence List:

1. How to flirt without being obvious

2. Sexy but classy outfit choices

3. Body language that says "I'm interested"

4. What kind of bras/underwear men prefer

5. *How to kiss in a way that makes him want more*
6. *Grooming preferences (down there???)*
7. *How to make the first move w/o seeming desperate*
8. *The art of the BJ – technique questions*
9. *How to tell if he's into kinky things*
10. *Positions and what guys actually want in bed*

Jesus Christ. I run a hand through my hair and look up at Stella, who's still leaning against the counter like she's waiting for test results. Her cheeks are pink, but her chin is set in that determined way that means she's serious about this.

"Stella," I say carefully, "some of these things—"

"Are too personal?" she finishes, her Southern accent creeping in. "I know it's awkward, but Brandon, you have six sisters. You know what women worry about. And you're..." She waves her hand vaguely in my direction. "You know. Experienced."

"Experienced," I repeat dryly.

"Don't make me spell it out. You date. A lot. Successfully." She leans forward, her hands clasped. "I'm offering to return the favor, you know. Whatever you need help with. Work stuff, personal assistant tasks. I'll organize your entire life if you want."

I suddenly feel the weight of everything I've been carrying. She waits, and something about her patience makes the words tumble out.

"You mentioned something about other career options for me. I'm wondering if—"

"Yes, I can totally help you with that!"

"This shoulder thing has me sidelined, and I'm starting to think about what comes next." I walk over to the couch and hear her soft steps follow. "The truth is, I have no idea what I'd do if I can't perform stunts anymore. My dad keeps hinting about coming back to New York to work in the family business, but that feels like giving up on everything I've built here."

Stella's expression shifts to what I recognize as her professional mode. "Are you kidding me? Brandon, you have so many options within the industry."

"Like what? Once my body can't handle the physical demands anymore, I don't know what to do."

"It doesn't mean your career in this field has to be over." She sits on the couch next to me and pulls her legs up under her. "You don't just disappear when you age out of performing. Let me help you. This is what I do."

I look at her, filled with skepticism...but maybe with a side of hope.

"Stunt coordination, choreography. You could develop safety protocols or train the next generation." Her excitement is infectious. "Brandon, you have over a decade of experience, relationships throughout the industry, and an understanding of both the creative and technical sides. You wouldn't be starting over, either. It would be a natural evolution."

The way she talks about it, with such clarity and confidence, makes something ease in my chest.

"You'd really help me explore that?"

"Of course. We can research opportunities, make connections, create a plan that keeps you in Hollywood but positions you for longevity." She grins. "I'm very good at what I do."

"Deal," I say, meaning it. "And you have to promise me something."

"What?"

"You don't tell anyone about the shoulder concerns. Not the girls, not anyone. I'm not ready for that conversation yet."

She mimes zipping her lips. "Promise."

I pick up her list again, feeling like we've shifted into more honest territory. "Some of this stuff..." I point to items eight through ten. "It's graduate-level material, and you're still in intro classes."

She deflates slightly. "But what if—"

"Stella. Trust the process." I give her a look.

She nods reluctantly.

"Alright, let's talk about what actually matters when you're trying to catch someone's attention." I lean back against the couch, studying her face. "But first, can I ask you something?"

"Oh, we're starting this now?" She reaches for her notebook. "I thought we were going to ease into the lesson part."

"No time like the present." I shift closer, my voice dropping. "Why do you show up completely differently in your personal life than you do at work?"

"What do you mean?"

"I mean, I've seen you walk into a conference room. You make eye contact with everyone, you choose the seat that gives you the best vantage point, you speak up, you tell stories." I gesture toward her current position, curled up in the corner of the couch. "But put you in a social setting, and suddenly, you're shrinking into corners, avoiding eye contact, waiting for someone else to start conversations."

Her cheeks flush pink, and I catch her unconsciously straightening her posture.

"I've watched women work a room before. The ones who get noticed aren't necessarily the prettiest ones. They're the ones who show up like they belong there." I think about the women who've caught my attention over the years. "There was this girl at a wrap party last month. She walked in and immediately scanned the room like she was assessing the landscape. Made eye contact, chose her spot strategically, joined conversations instead of waiting to be included. Every guy in the room gravitated toward her."

"What did she do differently?"

"She showed up the same way you do in a boardroom. Confident, present, like she had every right to be there." I lean forward. "Stella, you're beautiful. But more than that, you're smart and funny and competitive as hell. Why don't you let people see that version of you?"

Her breath catches slightly at the admission.

"That's what Mason, or that guy from last night, or any guy you like, needs to see. Not some shrinking-violet version of yourself, but the woman who negotiates million-dollar deals and isn't afraid to fight for what she wants."

She looks up from her notebook. "Okay, but can we talk about the touching thing? I felt like those women were touching you all night. How do I know when it's okay to touch a guy?"

I have to take a sip of my coffee before answering because my brain immediately goes to all the times she's touched me without thinking about it. "Read his body language first. If he's standing close to you, if he seems relaxed and engaged."

"Okay, but explain it specifically. What did you do to make those girls touch you?"

"Start small." My voice comes out rougher than I intended. "When you're laughing at something he said, let your hand rest on his forearm for just a second. Not a grab, just a light touch."

I demonstrate by brushing my fingers against her arm, and I feel her slight intake of breath.

"You do that sometimes," I continue, pulling my hand back. "When you're excited about something or trying to make a point." I clear my throat. "If we were actually dating, that would drive me completely insane."

Her pen hovers over the notebook. "Good insane or bad insane?"

"Good. Definitely good." I lean back, trying to create some distance. "Or when you bite your lip when you're concentrating. You probably don't even realize you do it, but it's distracting as hell."

"I bite my lip?"

"All the time. During *Love Island*, when you're analyzing someone's body language. When you're reading contracts." I take another sip of coffee. "Trust me, guys will notice."

She's staring at me now with an expression I can't quite read, her notebook forgotten in her lap.

"The most important thing is to remember who you are," I continue, forcing myself back on track. "Don't try to be someone else."

"Thank you," she says quietly. "I know this is probably weird, asking you to teach me how to touch other people."

"It's not weird." I lean forward, making sure she's looking

at me. "You're just being strategic about something you want. That's very you."

"But you probably think I should just be myself, and if a guy doesn't like it, then forget him."

"I think you should absolutely be yourself. But there's nothing wrong with wanting to put your best foot forward." I gesture at her notebook. "This is just confidence building. You already have everything you need, and we're just making sure you know how to use it."

seventeen

. . .

Stella

THE BEVERLY HILLS spa feels like stepping into a cloud made of eucalyptus and expensive skincare products. My mother practically floats through the reception area in her perfectly coordinated athleisure outfit, already chatting with the hostess about which treatments will be "absolutely divine" for mother-daughter bonding.

"This is exactly what we needed," she says, linking her arm through mine as we're led to the relaxation lounge. "Some proper girl time without any distractions."

By distractions, she means Brandon, who's probably sprawled across his couch right now with a baseball game on in the background, his phone propped up for one of his marathon FaceTime calls with his family. He's blissfully unaware that he's about to become the primary topic of conversation for the next four hours.

We settle into plush robes with cucumber water and wait for our first treatment, and I can practically see my mother's mental checklist forming as we settle into the zero gravity relaxation chairs.

"So," she begins, and I brace myself. "Brandon seems absolutely smitten with you. The way he was looking at you at dinner, touching your hand, making sure you were comfortable."

"Mama, we've only been dating a few weeks."

"Honey, when you know, you know. And that boy knows." She takes a delicate sip of her cucumber water. "The question is, do you know? Because a man like Brandon isn't going to wait around forever while you figure out your feelings."

There it is. The subtle pressure wrapped in maternal concern that's been my constant companion since I was old enough to date.

"I care about him a lot," I say carefully, which isn't even a lie. "But I'm not ready to start planning our future after a few weeks."

"Haven't you been hanging out longer than that, though?" Her voice takes on that gentle but firm tone I remember from childhood lectures about proper behavior. "A strong foundation of friendship makes the best marriages."

"Marriage?" The word comes out higher than I intended.

"Well, not immediately, of course. But Stella, you're twenty-five. You can't just date for fun forever. At some point, you need to think about building a life with someone."

I feel that familiar tightness in my chest, the same feeling I get whenever she starts talking about timelines and life plans like they're train schedules I'm already running late for.

"What if I'm not ready to build a life with anyone? What if I want to focus on my career for a few more years?"

"Your career is lovely, sugar, but it's not going to keep you warm at night, give you children, or take care of you when you're older." She reaches over and pats my hand. "Besides, Brandon seems very understanding about your work."

"What if I don't want children?" The words slip out before I can stop them, and my mother's face goes through a series of expressions that would be comical if they weren't so telling. It's not that I don't want children. I might. I'm trying to make a point here, though.

"What do you mean you don't want children? Of course you want children. Every woman wants children."

"Not every woman, Mama. Some women are perfectly happy focusing on their careers, their relationships, their own lives without adding children to the mix."

"That's just something young women say before they meet the right man and realize what they're missing." Her voice has that patient tone she uses when she thinks I'm being silly. "Trust me, once you settle down with Brandon and start thinking about the future, your maternal instincts will kick in."

The assumption that I'll automatically want different things once I'm with the "right man" makes me want to scream. Like my current feelings and desires are just place-holders until a man comes along to show me what I really want.

"What if they don't, though? What if I'm one of those women who's genuinely happy without kids?"

My mother sets down her cucumber water and really

looks at me for the first time since we sat down. "Stella Suzanne, where is this coming from? You've always been so good with children. You babysat for the neighbors. You volunteered at the church nursery."

"Being good with children and wanting to spend my life raising them are two different things."

She's quiet for a moment, and I can see her processing this information like it's a foreign language she's trying to translate.

"When I was your age," she says finally, her voice softer than usual, "I wanted to be a teacher."

The admission catches me completely off guard. In twenty-five years, I've never heard my mother express interest in any career beyond being a wife and mother.

"You did?"

"Elementary school. I had this whole plan worked out. I was going to teach second grade, help children learn to read, maybe work my way up to being a principal someday." There's something wistful in her voice that I've never heard before. "I even got accepted to the education program at the University of Georgia."

"What happened?"

"I met your father." She smiles, but there's something complicated in it. "He was so charming, so sure about what he wanted. And what he wanted was a wife who could support his career, host dinner parties, raise his children. He made it sound like such an adventure, building a life together."

"Do you regret giving up teaching?"

She considers this for a long moment. "I wouldn't change

having you, of course. You're the best thing I ever did. But sometimes, I wonder what kind of teacher I would have been. Whether I could have made a difference in children's lives."

The vulnerability in her admission makes my chest tight. This is the most real conversation we've had in years, maybe ever.

"You could still teach, you know. It's never too late to go back and get your teaching certificate."

"Oh, honey, that ship sailed long ago. I'm fifty-two years old, and your father needs me to handle the social aspects of his business. It's a full-time job keeping up with all the entertaining and charity work."

The way she dismisses her dreams so casually breaks my heart a little.

"But that's exactly why I'm telling you this," she continues, her voice taking on that familiar urgency. "Life is hard for women, sweetheart. We have to make difficult choices that men never have to think about. That's why it's so important to find someone who can take care of you, who can give you security so you don't have to sacrifice everything."

And just like that, we're back to where we started. The brief glimpse of the woman my mother might have been disappears behind the same old advice about finding security through a man.

"But what if I want to take care of myself? What if I want to build my own security?"

"You can't build security the way men can, Stella. The world simply doesn't work that way for us." She reaches for my hand again, and there's something sharper in her voice now, less sugar-sweet and more matter-of-fact. "I've watched too many women pour everything into their careers, thinking independence means doing it all alone. They end up exhausted, passed over for promotions, struggling to keep up with men who don't have to worry about biological clocks or being seen as too aggressive.

"The system isn't fair, sweetheart. A man can focus entirely on his career because that's what he's supposed to do. But a woman? She's fighting an uphill battle. I'm not saying you can't have interests or ambitions. I'm saying, why struggle and sacrifice when you could find a good man who wants to take care of you? Let him handle the pressure of being the provider. You could still work if you wanted to, but you wouldn't have to. You'd have choices, security, and a life that isn't consumed by climbing a ladder that was never meant for women in the first place."

The therapist calls our name for our couples massage, saving me from having to respond. As we're led to the treatment room, I can't shake the image of my twenty-two-year-old mother, excited about teaching second-graders, giving up her dreams because she thought she had to choose.

But what bothers me more is the realization that she might be trying to live vicariously through my choices, still hoping I'll accept the traditional path she chose and validate that she made the right decision all those years ago. The problem is, I'm not sure I want the kind of security that requires giving up pieces of myself to get it.

As the massage therapists work out the tension in our shoulders, I find myself thinking about Brandon. About how he supports my career without trying to minimize it. About how he listens when I talk about work like it actually matters.

About how he's never once suggested that my goals should be secondary to his.

Maybe my mother's right that Brandon is a good man. But maybe she's wrong about why that matters.

Maybe the point isn't finding someone to take care of me. Maybe it's finding someone who believes I'm capable of taking care of myself.

eighteen

. . .

Brandon

IT'S day four of living with Stella, and her mother has extended her stay. She's said something about wanting to spend more quality time with us as a couple. What started as a few days of fake boyfriend duty is stretching into a week of domestic intimacy that's messing with my head.

The problem isn't that Stella's staying at my place. It's how much I like having her at my place. How right it feels to wake up knowing she's in my bed, to hear her humming in the shower, to find her coffee mug next to mine in the sink. After that kiss at the restaurant and that damn list she made, I can't even look at her without my brain going places it absolutely shouldn't.

So, here I am at seven in the morning, forcing myself through shoulder rehab exercises in the building's gym, because staying in the apartment while she gets ready for work is becoming a special kind of torture. I need the distraction, and I need to get my head straight before I do something stupid.

The shoulder-press machine is mocking me. Three months ago, I could've knocked this weight out without breaking a sweat. Now I'm gritting my teeth halfway through the second set, too stubborn to admit how far I've backslid.

I'm debating one more rep when Mason walks in.

He's already in workout gear, his earbuds slung around his neck, looking like someone who actually plans his workouts instead of using the gym to escape his feelings.

"Morning," he says, grabbing a towel off the rack.

"Hey, Mason."

"Early start today?" He settles onto the bench next to the machine I'm using, clearly in no rush to begin his own workout.

"Yeah, couldn't sleep. Figured I'd get some energy out."

"I feel you. I've been up since five working on this app." He stretches his shoulders. "Sometimes, I think I spend more time in front of a computer than I do sleeping."

"What kind of app?"

"Adoption matching for animal shelters. Trying to streamline the whole process, make it easier for people to find the right pet." His face lights up as he talks about it.

"That's cool, man. Noble cause."

"Thanks. It's one of those things where, if it works, it could really make a difference, you know?" He pauses, fidgeting with his towel. "Hey, random question, but you're friends with Stella, right? The girl from our building?"

"Yeah."

"Are you guys, like, together? A couple or something?"

I'm not sure how to respond to that question at this exact moment, but the odds of Mason running into Stella's mom or seeing us together are slim. "Nah, just good friends. She lives across the hall, and we sort of run in the same circles professionally."

"Cool." He takes a sip from his water bottle. "What does she do again? I know she's always dressed really sharp."

"She's a talent agent."

His eyebrows shoot up. "No shit? That's awesome. Does she know famous people?"

There's something about the way his face lights up that rubs me wrong. Like Stella just became more interesting because of who she might know instead of who she is.

"Some, yeah. It's her job."

"That's so cool. I bet she can get passes to movie premieres and stuff, right?" He grins like he's joking, but there's genuine interest behind it. "Must be nice having connections like that."

I shrug, not liking where this is going. "She works hard for her clients."

"Oh, totally. I'm sure she's great at what she does." He starts setting up at the bench press. "She just seems so, I don't know, shy? I'll say hey in the hallway, and she practically runs away. It's kind of cute, actually."

"She's just not great with small talk." I try to reel in the defensiveness that I'm sure is coming out in my voice.

"That's surprising, though, right? I mean, with a career like hers, wouldn't networking and client schmoozing be a huge part of the job?" He loads weights onto the bar, his tone genuinely curious but missing the mark. "I bet, once she gets comfortable, she's probably totally different. You know how some people are just quiet at first, then they open up."

The casual confidence in his voice makes my jaw clench. Like Stella's selectiveness is just shyness that needs to be coaxed out of her rather than her being deliberate about who she lets in.

But maybe I'm being unfair. Maybe my own feelings are making me read too much into innocent comments. Mason seems like a decent-enough guy on the surface. He's successful, confident, and obviously, there's some interest in Stella. Just because he's not expressing himself the way I would doesn't mean he's bad for her.

"You been living here long?" Mason asks, moving to adjust his weights.

"Almost four years. You?"

"Just hit the one-year mark. Love the location, hate the rent." He laughs, and it's genuine enough. "But being this close to work makes it worth it. My office is literally a ten-minute walk, which is a miracle in this city."

"Yeah, the commute thing is huge."

"Exactly. Plus, the building's got good people. Friendly neighbors, you know? You, Stella." He adjusts his grip on the bar, then pauses. "She seems nice. Really nice."

I keep my expression neutral, waiting to see where this is going.

"I just feel like every time I run into her, she's rushing off somewhere. Always seems busy." He does another rep, his tone carefully casual. "Probably just has a lot going on with work and everything."

There's something in the way he says it, like he's fishing for information without wanting to seem too interested.

"Maybe you could put in a good word for me?" The

request comes out more hesitant than before. "I mean, just so she knows I'm not some weirdo or anything."

I want to tell him no. That Stella's too good for him, that he should look elsewhere. But then I remember her asking for my help, remember how her face lit up when she talked about wanting to get Mason's attention.

"Sure, I can do that."

Maybe I'm the problem here. Maybe I'm seeing red flags where there aren't any because the thought of Stella with someone else makes me want to punch something.

"You know, you should just talk to her more," I say, forcing the words out. "She's actually pretty easy to get along with once you get past the initial shyness."

"Yeah?" Mason brightens as he towels off his hands. "Actually, there's this trivia thing my office does on Wednesday nights. Pretty casual, just a bunch of us from work meeting up at this bar near downtown."

He pauses, like he's working up the courage for something.

"Think she'd be into that?"

Something clicks. This could be perfect for Stella. If she wants Mason's attention, trivia would be right in her wheelhouse. She'd destroy the competition, and he'd see exactly how brilliant she is.

"You should definitely mention it if you get the chance. She's incredible at trivia. Like, scary good."

"Really?" Mason's interest is immediate and obvious, and I can practically see the wheels turning in his head. "That could be the perfect icebreaker. Maybe next time I see her in the hallway, I'll ask."

The enthusiasm in his voice should make me happy. But for some reason, it doesn't.

"Enjoy the rest of your workout. I need to get ready for work." I exit the gym before Mason can say anything else or before I totally lose my cool and tell him to stay away from her.

When I get back to my apartment, there's a bright yellow Post-it stuck to the coffee maker in Stella's neat handwriting.

Took Mom to the studio for a tour, then dinner after.
Made you a sandwich for lunch – it's in the fridge.
You're on your own tonight!
– S

I stare at the note longer than I should, my chest doing something weird at the casual domesticity of it all. She made me lunch. Left me a note. Thought about my day while she was planning hers.

And now, with the advice and tips I shared with Mason, I feel like I just pushed Stella away when I'm starting to feel like I don't want to let her go.

nineteen

. . .

Brandon

"YOU LOOK NICE," I say, leaning against the doorframe as I watch Stella tidy my bed with careful precision. "Big plans this morning?"

She's fully dressed and clearly operating on multiple cups of coffee, wearing dark jeans that actually fit her curves instead of hiding them, paired with a soft pink sweater that makes her eyes look impossibly blue. Her hair falls in loose waves around her shoulders, and there's something apologetic about the way she's smoothing my comforter.

"Coffee. With my mom." She fluffs the pillows one more time before turning to face me. "I'm really sorry, but I need to borrow my boyfriend for an hour."

"Let me check my call time—"

"You don't have to be there until eleven." She's already moving to straighten the items on my nightstand, clearly feeling guilty about commandeering my space. "I already checked. I'm sorry for being presumptuous."

"You checked my schedule?" I can't help but grin. "That's very girlfriend-like of you."

"Don't get smart with me." But she's fighting a smile as she adjusts my alarm clock. "She keeps asking when she'll see you again, and coffee seemed like the most painless option. Quick, public, minimal opportunities for embarrassing stories about my childhood."

I watch her fuss over my nightstand, trying to leave it exactly as she found it, and something warm spreads through my chest. She's been staying here for days, but she's still treating my space like she's a guest who doesn't want to overstep.

"You know you don't have to put everything back perfectly, right? You're allowed to exist here."

"I just don't want to mess up your routine." She pauses, biting her lip. "And I really am sorry for volunteering you. I was hoping I could get away with vague boyfriend references, but she's more persistent than I anticipated."

"Give me five minutes to change into something that screams 'worthy of your daughter.'"

When I emerge in dark jeans and a navy henley, Stella's waiting by the door, looking relieved rather than terrified.

"Perfect timing!"

We both turn as Caroline appears from Stella's apartment. Despite the early hour, she looks like she stepped out of a *Southern Living* magazine. Her cream cardigan is perfectly pressed, and she's practically glowing with anticipation.

"Good morning, Caroline," I say, automatically reaching for Stella's hand. "Ready for some coffee?"

"Oh, I've been looking forward to this!" Caroline's face lights up as she takes in our coordinated casual outfits. "And look at you two! You match without even trying. Isn't that sweet?"

Stella squeezes my hand once, a silent thank you for playing along.

"I found the most charming little café just around the corner," Caroline continues, already heading to the elevator. "Perfect for getting to know my daughter's boyfriend better."

As we follow her, I lean close to Stella's ear. "See? Painless."

"We haven't gotten to the interrogation part yet," she murmurs back.

This should be fun.

As we round the corner toward the café, I catch sight of a familiar figure through the window: Mason, sitting at a table near the front, laptop open, completely absorbed in whatever he's working on.

Stella sees him at the exact same moment, and her grip on my hand tightens. I can practically feel her panic over the situational shit show we're in. We're meant to be boyfriend and girlfriend in front of her mother, but not at all in front of Mason.

That's when I spot our salvation in the form of a small table in the back corner that's about to be vacated by a couple gathering their things.

"You know what, Caroline?" I say, smoothly guiding us toward the door while dropping Stella's hand as naturally as possible. "Why don't you grab that table before someone else does? Stella and I can handle the coffee orders."

"Great idea," Caroline says.

Stella shoots me a look of pure gratitude as her mother heads to the back table, completely oblivious to the fact that she's just been expertly maneuvered away from witnessing whatever's about to happen between her daughter and Mason.

"You're a genius," Stella whispers.

"Just don't let me down," I whisper back, giving her a gentle push toward the counter.

The coffee shop is exactly what you'd expect from a place that charges seven dollars for a latte. Exposed brick, plants hanging from the ceiling, the kind of carefully curated, rustic vibe that screams, "We're artisanal!" It's busy enough that we won't stand out, but not so packed that we can't move around.

"Oh, God, he looks really good. Is that a new shirt?"

"It's a gray t-shirt, Stell. Pretty standard."

"But it fits him really well."

I glance over. She's not wrong. Mason looks like he was designed by someone with excellent taste in men.

"You ready?" I ask.

Stella nods, but she's holding my hand again, and the grip says she has no intention of letting go anytime soon.

"I think it might look better if you let go of my hand."

"Oh, shit. I'm sorry." She looks up at me, and for a minute, neither of us makes a move to untangle from each other. It's like, for a moment, we both realize how natural this feels.

We reach the counter, and Stella orders. While we wait for our coffee, I can see her shoulders starting to tense up again, so I place my hand on her back, just between her shoulder blades, and give her neck a gentle squeeze.

"Breathe, sunshine," I murmur, quiet enough that only she can hear. "You've got this."

She relaxes slightly under my touch, and I feel her take a deeper breath.

"Stella," the barista calls out. She takes her drink, turns around with what she probably thinks is casual surprise, and stops mid-step. Mason has looked up from his laptop and is staring directly at her.

"Oh! Hi, Mason," she says, her voice about an octave higher than usual. "I didn't see you there."

He smiles, the kind of warm, genuine smile that makes it obvious why Stella's been obsessing over this guy. "Hey, Stella. Nice to see you outside the building."

"Yeah, I love this place. The coffee's great." She gestures vaguely with her cup. "This is my friend Brandon. Brandon, this is Mason."

I bite back a grin as Mason stands, clearly entertained. "Good to see you again, man."

"Right," Stella says, her voice a whisper. "You two know each other."

"Likewise." I turn to Stella with a grin. "That reminds me. I mentioned to Mason that you're a trivia whiz."

Mason's face lights up. "He did! And I wanted to see if you would be interested in trivia tomorrow night? Eight o'clock at 33 Taps. Feel free to bring friends if you want to. It's more fun with a lot of people."

Stella's face brightens immediately. "I love trivia! That sounds really fun."

"Great. I hope you'll come." He starts packing up his laptop. "I should probably get going, but I'm really glad we ran into each other."

"Me, too!" Stella says, her voice still pitched slightly higher than normal.

He waves goodbye and heads out, giving us both a friendly nod as he passes. I watch Stella track his movement through the window until he disappears from view. Then she turns back to me with a grimace.

"Well?" I ask as we make our way back toward Caroline's table.

She slumps slightly, her shoulders deflating. "That was terrible. I was so awkward."

"You were fine. A little nervous, maybe, but he didn't seem to notice."

"He invited me to trivia but said I could bring friends. That's not exactly romantic."

"It's an opening. First contact. You build from there."

We reach Caroline's table and settle into our chairs. She looks up from her phone with mild curiosity.

"Who was that handsome young man you were talking to, dear?"

"Just a neighbor from our building," Stella says, reaching for her coffee.

Caroline's eyebrows lift slightly. "Well, I hope you made it clear you're not available. He seemed to be flirting with you."

Stella's eyes find mine across the small table, and something in her expression shifts. Her hand slides across the table to cover mine, and our fingers intertwine with a naturalness that catches me off guard.

"Don't worry, Mama," she says as her thumb traces my knuckles. "I know exactly what I want."

Her voice is soft, meant for her mother, but her eyes stay locked on mine. There's something in her gaze that makes my chest tight.

"Brandon's the only man I'm interested in getting to know better."

The way she says it, still holding my gaze, makes it impossible to tell where the performance ends and something real begins. Her fingers tighten slightly around mine, and for a moment, I forget we're supposed to be pretending.

My thumb traces across her knuckles without conscious thought, and I watch her pupils dilate slightly in response. The space between us feels electric.

Slowly, reluctantly, she turns back to her mother, but her hand stays tangled with mine on the table. Her fingers squeeze gently, and I'm left wondering if that declaration was purely for Caroline's benefit or if there was something real underneath that perfectly delivered performance.

Because nothing about the way she said it felt like part of our charade.

twenty

. . .

Stella

BY THE TIME I make it back to Brandon's apartment, it's almost ten o'clock at night, and I'm emotionally drained from the day. Between the coffee shop this morning, work this afternoon, and then dinner with my mother, I'm exhausted.

I kick off my heels the moment I'm through the door and immediately collapse onto Brandon's couch with a dramatic sigh. "I love my mother, but I feel like I just performed a one-woman show for three hours straight."

"She's thorough, I'll give her that," Brandon says, settling beside me and reaching for the remote. "What do you want to watch? Something that doesn't require thinking?"

"Actually," I say, curling my legs under me and turning to face him, "I was wondering if we could work on some things from my list tonight."

He pauses with the remote halfway to the coffee table, and I catch something flicker across his expression that I can't quite read.

"Which things?" he asks, his voice carefully neutral.

"Well, trivia night is tomorrow." I pull my hair over one shoulder, suddenly feeling nervous about bringing this up. "Maybe we could practice some of the flirting techniques you mentioned? Like, how do I let Mason know I'm attracted to him without literally saying, 'You're so hot'?"

"Oh, that's easy. Body language," he says immediately. "We talked about it the other night. Eye contact, finding excuses to touch him casually."

"Ohmygod, that's so easy! Why didn't I think of that?" I say, the sarcasm dripping from my lips.

"It really is, though." Brandon shifts to face me on the couch. "You probably do a lot of it instinctively."

"Okay, but I need you to spell it out for me. What are the big things I need to make sure I'm doing?"

"Eye contact first. When someone's talking to you, really look at them. Not just polite listening but like you're genuinely fascinated by what they're saying."

"Show me."

"What?"

"Show me the difference. Look at me like you're being polite. Then look at me like you're fascinated."

He gives me a standard smile, the kind he probably uses with people he meets at work. Pleasant, friendly, but forgettable. Then something shifts in his expression. His eyes focus on mine with an intensity that makes my stomach flutter, like I'm the most interesting person he's ever encountered.

"Oh," I say, feeling my cheeks warm. "Yeah, I can see the difference."

"Good. Now you try it on me."

I attempt to replicate what he just did, focusing on his

eyes and trying to project genuine interest. It feels awkward at first, but his eyes dart off to the side, and I know I'm getting somewhere.

"Better," he says, his voice rougher than it was a moment ago. "But don't overthink it. The key is to actually be interested, not to perform interest."

I nod, filing that away. "Okay, so how do I find ways to touch him but not in a creepy way?"

"Just nothing obvious, small moments of contact that create connection." He demonstrates by reaching over to brush an imaginary piece of lint off my shoulder. The brief contact sends electricity down my arm. "Or, if he says something funny, you might touch his arm while you laugh."

His hand is still resting on my shoulder, and I'm suddenly very aware of the warmth of his palm through my sweater.

"Like this?" I reach over and place my hand on his forearm, letting my fingers linger just long enough to feel his muscles tense under my touch.

"Exactly like that," he says, but his voice is softer.

We're sitting close enough that I can see his whiskey-colored eyes, can smell his cologne mixed with the faint scent of whatever soap he uses. For a second, I forget we're supposed to be practicing for Mason.

"What else?" I ask, not moving my hand.

"You could copy his body language," he says, seeming to refocus. "If he leans in, you lean in. If he crosses his arms, you cross yours. It creates subconscious connection."

"Does it work?"

"Try it."

Brandon leans back against the couch cushions, and I

mirror the movement. He tilts his head slightly to the right, and I do the same. There's something hypnotic about following his movements, like we're dancing without music.

"Huh, I've never even thought about doing that," I admit.

"It works," he says, and there's something in his voice that makes me look at him more carefully. "Your body language right now is telling me you're engaged, interested, maybe a little nervous but in a good way."

"How so?" I ask, genuinely curious.

"You're leaning toward me instead of away. Your pupils are dilated. You're touching your hair, which usually means someone's feeling self-conscious but not uncomfortable." His eyes drop to my lips for just a moment before meeting my gaze again. "It's all very attractive."

The word hangs between us, and I feel heat creep up my neck. "So, this would work on Mason?"

"This would work on any man with a pulse," he says quietly.

"Okay, let's talk about what I should wear."

"Whatever you feel the most confident in."

I have to think about that. "There was this dress I wore to Natalie's birthday party last year. Black, fitted, with this square neckline that showed just enough without being scandalous. I felt...powerful in it."

"I remember that dress," Brandon says immediately.

"You do?"

"Trust me, every guy at that party remembers that dress. You looked incredible."

"Really?" I feel ridiculously pleased by this. "I thought maybe it was too much."

"It was perfect. You walked in, and the entire room noticed. I watched at least three guys work up the courage to come talk to you."

"I had no idea."

"Oh, sunshine, if you could only see the effect you have on people." There's something in his voice that makes me study his face more carefully. I'm suddenly aware of how close we're sitting, how his hand is still resting on the back of the couch near my shoulder.

"What else do you want to know?" Brandon says, breaking the spell.

"Right." I clear my throat. "I guess tell me what I don't know."

"Well, you know that being confident is key, but that confidence comes from knowing what you want and not being afraid to go after it."

"What if I don't know what I want?"

"You do know." His voice drops lower, more certain. "You're just scared to admit it."

"How can you be so sure?"

"Because I watch you make decisions all day long. You know exactly what you want when it comes to your clients, your career, your life." He adjusts his position, too, angling toward me until our knees are almost touching. "The only time you second-guess yourself is when it comes to this."

"This?"

"Going after something that matters to you personally instead of professionally."

The way he's looking at me makes my skin feel too warm. Like he can see something I'm not ready to acknowledge.

"The trick is learning to trust your instincts instead of overthinking everything," he continues, his voice quieter now.

"My instincts?" The word comes out breathier than I intended.

"Like right now." He leans forward slightly, closing the space between us by inches. "What are your instincts telling you to do?"

The question hangs in the air. I can smell his cologne, something clean and masculine that makes me want to lean closer. His eyes drop to my lips for just a fraction of a second before meeting mine again.

My heart is beating so hard that I'm sure he can hear it. The honest answer is that my instincts are screaming at me to close the remaining distance between us, to put my lips on his again and forget all about Mason and trivia night and everything except the way Brandon is looking at me right now.

"I should probably go get ready for bed," I whisper instead.

"Probably," he agrees, but his voice is rough around the edges now.

Neither of us moves. The space between us feels electric, charged with something I don't have words for. His hand is resting on the back of the couch, close enough that if I shifted just slightly, his fingers would brush my shoulder.

I force myself to stand, my legs unsteady. "Good night, Brandon."

"Night, Stella."

I can feel his eyes following me as I cross to his bedroom. When I reach the doorway, I risk a glance back and find him still watching me, his expression unreadable in the dim light.

In the bedroom, I close the door behind me and lean against it, my heart still racing. I head to the small section of his closet where I've hung a few clothes.

I pull out a few options, but my mind keeps drifting to the black dress with the square neckline. The one that made Brandon notice me at Natalie's party. The one that made him remember exactly how I looked, almost a year later. I shake my head and focus. Trivia at a dive bar calls for something more casual.

But as I settle on dark jeans and a fitted emerald top that brings out my eyes, I can't help but wonder why Brandon's opinion suddenly seems to matter more than Mason's.

twenty-one

Stella

I PACE OUTSIDE 33 TAPS, adjusting my top. The soft fabric hugs my curves just right, and paired with my favorite dark jeans and ankle boots, I feel good.

"Stella, you're going to wear a hole in the sidewalk," Natalie says as she walks up to meet me. She grabs my arm to stop my pacing. "And your shoes are too cute to ruin."

I convinced Natalie to join me tonight since Mason suggested I bring a friend, which I hated but am now very grateful for.

"I'm just excited," I say. And I am. This is what I wished for. I had to set Mom up with tickets to that new musical just so I could have tonight free, but it'll be worth it if I can finally connect with Mason.

"Good excited or nervous excited?" Natalie asks as we head toward the entrance.

"Good excited, I think."

The bar is packed when we walk in, a mix of young professionals and locals. The trivia setup takes up most of the back half of the space, with mismatched tables and chairs scattered around a small stage where someone's testing the sound system.

I scan the room and spot Mason immediately. He's sitting at a corner booth with a large group of people, and my stomach drops when I realize that at least five of them are women. Gorgeous women. Women with perfectly tousled beach hair, effortless makeup, and the confident body language that suggests they've never doubted their place in a room.

"There he is," I whisper to Natalie, nodding toward the booth.

"The tall guy in the blue button-down?"

"That's him."

"Oh, he's cute! Not quite Brandon hot, but I can see why you'd like him."

I'm not sure how to take that comment, so I leave it alone.

She studies the table for a moment. "Okay, so there are a lot of people. That's good. Less pressure. We'll just introduce ourselves and play it by ear."

Easy for her to say. She's not the one about to walk into what looks like a scene from a tech company's social media page, all beautiful people laughing at inside jokes while I stand here feeling like I'm about to crash a party I wasn't really invited to.

Mason notices me before I can lose my nerve completely. He waves me over with a genuine smile that makes my heart skip.

"Stella! You made it!" He stands to greet me, and I'm

reminded again of how tall he is. "Everyone, this is Stella, the trivia ace I told you about."

A chorus of hellos greets me, and I manage to smile and wave without tripping over my own feet. Mason introduces everyone, but I only catch about half the names because I'm too busy trying not to stare at the woman sitting closest to him. She's stunning in that effortless California way, with sun-streaked blonde hair and the kind of tan that suggests she spends her weekends hiking or surfing.

"This is Amy," Mason says when he gets to her, and something about the way he says it feels deliberately casual. Too casual. Like he's working to make it sound unimportant. "We work on the same team."

Amy smiles at me, and it seems genuine enough, but there's something in the way she looks at Mason that makes my chest tighten. The familiarity. The ease with which she touches his arm when she talks to him. And the way Mason doesn't seem to notice or mind.

"Stella, come sit next to me," Mason says, patting the spot beside him. "I want our trivia ace right in the strategy zone."

I slide into the booth next to him, trying to ignore how good he smells or how his thigh brushes against mine when he leans forward to grab his drink. Natalie settles in across from us, and I'm grateful that she's here because I can feel myself getting flustered by Mason's proximity.

My phone buzzes with a text.

BRANDON

How's it going, sunshine? Knocking them dead with that Southern charm?

I glance around to make sure no one's watching before typing back.

STELLA

> I guess fine? I'm sitting next to him, which is good, but there's a girl that keeps touching his arm and I can't tell if there's something there. These women are all gorgeous and seem to know him really well.

BRANDON

> Breathe. You're not competing. You're just being yourself and seeing if there's a connection.

STELLA

> Easy for you to say. You don't see these women. They look like they stepped out of a magazine.

BRANDON

> So do you.

BRANDON

> Stop comparing and start connecting.

The trivia host calls for attention, and I put my phone away, trying to focus on the game instead of my spiraling thoughts.

The first few rounds go well enough. General knowledge, pop culture, sports. Mason's team is clearly competitive, with everyone shouting out answers and debating the finer points of various topics. I manage to contribute a few correct answers, including one about country music that earns me an impressed look from Mason.

"I didn't know you were into country," he says during a break between rounds.

"Born and raised on it," I say, then immediately worry that sounds too Southern, too unsophisticated for his crowd.

But he smiles. "That's cool. Very authentic."

My phone buzzes again.

BRANDON

Update?

STELLA

He just complimented my country music knowledge, but nothing else yet.

The bubbles pop up and then disappear. It happens a few more times before he replies.

BRANDON

Doesn't mean he's not interested in you.
What's your gut telling you?

I glance at Mason, who's laughing at something the guy next to me said. My gut is telling me I'm in way over my head.

STELLA

I don't know that I can trust my gut when it's about me.

BRANDON

You predict every Love Island couple and navigate multi-million dollar deals and you can't read that room?

Before I can respond, another text comes through.

BRANDON

Let me help you then. You're hot, funny, kind, and so many other amazing things. If he's not directing his total attention toward you, he's a fucking idiot.

STELLA

You have to say that. You're my friend.

BRANDON

I don't have to say anything. I could've just said try to stay open and not to read too much into anything.

I don't have a response to that. He's managed to completely take my breath away through a silly text.

BRANDON

Don't sell yourself short. You're amazing.

STELLA

Thank you.

I'm still staring at the phone when Natalie nudges me, pulling me out of my overanalyzing spiral.

"You okay?"

I can't deal with her teasing me about Brandon, so I lie.

"Yeah, just work stuff. Sorry about that."

The next round is entertainment, and I actually do well, answering questions about Oscar winners and box office records. It's my wheelhouse, and for the first time all night, I feel confident.

"Damn, Stella," Mason says after I correctly identify the highest-grossing film of 1997. "You really know your stuff. You must be incredible at your job."

"Thanks," I say, feeling a flush of pride. "I do love what I do."

"I bet you know tons of famous people, right? Like, actual celebrities?" There's an eagerness in his voice that makes me slightly uncomfortable.

"Some, yeah. It comes with the territory."

"That's so cool." He leans forward slightly. "Do you get invited to all those exclusive events? Like premieres and after-parties?"

"Sometimes," I admit. "Industry events are part of the job."

"That must be incredible. I've always wondered what those parties are really like." His smile widens. "Maybe you could bring me sometime? I'd love to see that world."

There's something in the way he says it that makes me pause, but I force a smile. "Yeah, that could be fun."

"I didn't realize you were so competitive," Mason says with a grin.

"Well, when you're raised by a mother who insists you join cotillion and participate in tennis competitions, you learn to bring your A-game to everything," I say with a laugh, then immediately worry that sounds too privileged or Southern.

But Mason looks intrigued. "Tennis competitions? That's cool. I've been trying to get better at tennis, actually. I play at the club near here on Saturday mornings, but I'm pretty terrible."

My heart does a little flip. This is it. This is my opening.

"I could give you some pointers sometime," I offer, trying to sound casual. "I mean, if you want."

"Really? That would be awesome."

He's pulled away into an animated discussion about risk versus reward when the trivia host announces the final round. Somehow, our table has climbed into second place, just three points behind the leaders.

"Okay, team," Mason says, suddenly focused. "This is sudden death. One question, winner takes all."

The energy at our table shifts, and everyone leans in as the host clears his throat.

"Your final question is about geography. What is the only country that is also a continent?"

"Australia!" I say immediately, without thinking.

The entire table erupts in cheers, and Mason grins at me across the table. "Stella for the win!"

The group toasts, and Mason reaches across to clink his glass against mine first. "I'm having way more fun tonight than I expected," he says, his eyes locked on mine. "Maybe next time, it can be just the two of us."

My heart skips at the implication, but then he turns to toast the rest of the table. When he gets to Amy, his arm slides around her shoulders to pull her into the celebration, and something uncomfortable twists in my stomach.

As the excitement dies down and people settle their tabs, the crowd thins out. I'm digging through my purse for my wallet when Mason appears beside me.

"Hey," he says, his voice quieter now that we're not competing anymore. "That was really fun. Thanks for helping us absolutely crush the competition."

"It was fun," I admit, surprised by how natural this conversation feels. "Your teammates are really nice."

"They liked you, too. You'll have to come back soon."

"Anytime," I say, surprised by how natural this feels now.

He pulls out his phone. "Let me get your number. I'll text you about tennis."

After we exchange numbers, he gives me a quick hug goodbye, and then he's gone, walking out with Amy and a few others from his group.

"So?" Natalie appears beside me as we head toward the door, her purse slung over her shoulder. "How was that? You looked like you actually had fun instead of analyzing everything."

"It was good, I think. Great, actually." I push open the door, and we step out into the cool night air. "He asked me to play tennis with him."

"Mm-hmm." There's something in her tone that makes me look at her sideways.

"What's that supposed to mean?"

"Nothing. I'm glad you had a good time." But she's got that expression she gets when she's thinking something she's not ready to share yet.

For the first time in months, I actually had a normal conversation with Mason without completely embarrassing myself. I didn't freeze up, I contributed to the team, and I even made him laugh a couple of times. That has to count for something.

But then there was that whole thing about the premieres. I hope he's not one of those guys who's more interested in what I can do for him than who I am. But maybe I'm overthinking it. Maybe he was just making conversation.

Which is fine. It's progress. It's just different from what I imagined.

twenty-two

. . .

Stella

I CAN HEAR the TV playing softly through Brandon's door as I fish my key out of my purse. When I let myself in, I find him sprawled on his couch in sweatpants and a t-shirt, with a half-empty beer on the coffee table and what looks like takeout containers from some burger place scattered around him.

"Hey," he says, muting the TV and sitting up when he sees me. "How did it go? You're back earlier than I expected."

"It was fine," I say, dropping my purse by the door and settling onto the couch beside him. The smell of fries and whatever burger he ordered makes my stomach rumble, reminding me that I barely touched the appetizers at trivia. Without thinking, I reach over and steal a handful of fries from his container.

"Just fine?" He watches as I chew, and amusement flickers across his face. "That doesn't sound like the ringing endorsement I was expecting."

With a shrug, I reach for more fries. "It was good. I didn't embarrass myself, which feels like a win. Mason was nice. His coworkers were friendly. I actually had fun once I stopped overthinking everything."

"But?" There's something in his tone that suggests he's picking up on my less-than-enthusiastic summary.

"But nothing. It was exactly what it was supposed to be." I pause, then remember why I was so eager to get back here. "Oh, before we get into all that, I have something for you."

I reach for my laptop bag and pull out both my computer and a folder thick with printed pages. "I was hoping to show you this before I left, but you were still on set when I had to go."

Brandon's eyebrows lift with curiosity as I open my laptop and start spreading papers across his coffee table, pushing aside his food to make room. "You've been busy," he says.

"I told you I'd help with your career transition, and I meant it." I open the folder and spread out several sheets of paper on his coffee table. "I've been researching, and Brandon, there are so many opportunities for someone with your experience."

He settles in next to me, close enough that I catch his familiar scent.

"Look at this," I say, pointing to a printed article. "Second-unit directors often come from stunt backgrounds. And here, Netflix just announced three new action series that'll need stunt coordinators. Plus, there's this whole emerging field of virtual production, where they need people who understand both physical action and digital environments."

As I walk him through my research, I feel that familiar

spark I get when I'm really in my element. This is what I love about my job: finding the perfect path forward, seeing possibilities that others might miss.

"You could start transitioning gradually," I continue, pulling up a spreadsheet I've created. "Take on more coordination responsibilities while you're still performing. Build relationships with directors and producers. I even found a mentorship program through the stunt coordinators' guild."

Brandon looks at me with an expression I can't quite read. "Stella, this is incredible. How long did you spend on this?"

"It was a slow day at work. It was nothing." I shrug. "Oh, that reminds me. We should go to Helena Voss's premiere tomorrow. Ava has a cameo role in it, so I can get us passes easily. Helena just sold a racing series, and it would be good for you to meet her."

"This isn't nothing," he says, digging through all the info I've gathered like it's Christmas. "This is fucking incredible."

Something warm spreads through my chest at the admiration in his voice. "It's really nothing. I actually love doing stuff like this."

"I can tell. You get this look when you talk about work, like you're exactly where you're supposed to be."

I smile at that. "It's funny because having my mother here this week has been interesting." I pause, trying to find the right words. "She sees my career as something I'm doing until I find my real purpose. Every conversation somehow circles back to marriage and babies, like all of this is just a phase I'll outgrow."

Brandon nods slowly. "I get that. My family loves me,

supports me completely, but they've never really understood why I'd choose this over joining the family business. They keep waiting for me to come to my senses and take my rightful place running hotels."

"Exactly!" I lean forward, feeling understood in a way I rarely do. "It's not that they don't want me to be happy. They just have a very specific blueprint for what happiness should look like."

"And they genuinely believe their way is better," he says with a knowing look. "Not malicious, just convinced they know what's best."

"Yes! And you feel guilty for wanting something different because you know how much they love you, how much they've given you." I shake my head. "It's hard to argue with people who want good things for you, even when their expectations don't quite fit."

We sit in comfortable silence for a moment, and I realize this is the most honest conversation I've had about my family in a long time. There's something about Brandon that makes me feel safe enough to admit things I don't usually say out loud.

"Speaking of expectations," I say, closing my laptop and turning to face him fully, "Can I get your thoughts on what goes through a guy's head on a first date?"

Brandon's eyes snap to mine. "Are you going on a date?"

"Well, Mason mentioned maybe playing tennis."

"Good for you!" Brandon shifts on the couch, reaching to pick up the papers I had spread out on the table. It feels like he's trying to avoid the question.

"So, what do guys want? What do they expect?"

Brandon is quiet for a moment.

"Those are two very different things," he says finally.

"What do you mean?"

"I mean what guys should expect versus what they'll probably want." He leans back into the couch and brings his knee up, turning to face me more fully. "What he should expect is for you to be yourself. To respect your boundaries. To treat you like the intelligent, accomplished woman you are. To pay for dinner because he asked you out. To walk you to your door. To not assume anything beyond that."

"And what he'll want?"

There's a shift in his eyes as his gaze moves across my face. "He'll want to know if you're as soft as you look. He'll want to know what you taste like, what sounds you make when someone touches you the right way."

My breath catches somewhere between my throat and my lungs. The rational part of my brain knows this is supposed to be educational, but the way he's looking at me right now doesn't feel like a lesson. It feels like a confession. Heat pools low in my belly, and I realize I'm leaning forward without meaning to, drawn by something magnetic in his voice.

"Oh." It's barely a whisper, but it's all I can manage.

"He'll want to know if you're the kind of woman who kisses on the first date," he continues, his voice dropping to that rough register that makes my skin feel too tight.

His hand moves from the back of the couch, and his fingers brush against my cheek as he tucks a strand of hair behind my ear. The contact sends electricity shooting down my spine. "If you're the kind of woman who lets a man take his time exploring every inch of your skin or the kind who takes control and shows him exactly what you want."

His touch lingers at my temple, and his thumb traces the shell of my ear. I can feel my pulse hammering against my throat and hear the slight change in his breathing. The space between us has shrunk to almost nothing, and I'm hyper-aware of everything—the warmth radiating from his chest, the way his eyes have gone dark, the faint hint of beer on his breath when he speaks.

My lips part slightly, and I watch his gaze drop to my mouth for just a heartbeat before meeting my eyes again. Every instinct I have is screaming at me to close the remaining distance between us.

"What kind of woman do you think I am?" I whisper.

The question hangs between us, loaded with meaning I'm not sure either of us is ready to acknowledge. Brandon's eyes are dark now, focused on me with an intensity that makes my skin feel too tight.

"I think," he says slowly, sliding his hand down my neck and resting on my shoulder, "that you're the kind of woman who surprises people. Who's stronger and braver and more passionate than anyone gives her credit for, including yourself."

His fingers trace my arm, and I can't suppress the small shiver that runs through me.

"I think you're the kind of woman who could drive a man completely out of his mind," he whispers.

We've somehow moved so close to each other that I can feel his breath against my lips. All it would take is the slightest movement, and our lips would be touching. My heart is beating so fast that I'm sure he can hear it.

"And how would I know you were interested in me that way?" I ask, the sound barely a whisper.

"Well, if I were interested in you—really interested—I'd make sure you knew I was thinking about you specifically." He slides one of my legs over his, moving us closer, facing one another. "I'd compliment you."

"Such as?"

His eyes travel over my face, taking in details like he's memorizing them. "Like how that green color of your shirt complements your skin. Or how your eyes get this little crinkle at the corners when you're really amused by something."

My cheeks warm under his attention. "What else?"

"I'd find excuses to touch you. Little touches that seem casual but aren't really casual at all."

His hand comes up to my face, and his thumb traces my cheek like he's wiping away something that isn't there. The contact sends heat shooting through me, and I have to remind myself that this is supposed to be educational.

"And then what?" I manage.

"Then I'd test the waters. See if you were receptive." His hand slides into my hair, and his fingers tangle gently in the strands. "If you didn't pull away, if you maybe leaned into the touch..."

I realize my body has shifted and I am leaning into his touch, my face tilting slightly up toward his. "Then what?"

"Then I'd know you were interested, too." His thumb

traces my jawline, and I feel my breath catch. "And maybe I'd take it a step further."

He shifts even closer, his hand slides to cup the back of my neck, and suddenly, we're much closer than we were a moment ago. The smell of his aftershave mixed with warm skin makes my head spin.

"How much further?" I whisper.

Instead of answering, he closes the distance between us and kisses me.

It starts soft, tentative, like he's giving me time to pull away. But when I kiss him back instead, something ignites between us. His mouth moves against mine with growing hunger, and I can taste the desperation in it, like he's been wanting this for longer than I realize.

My hands find their way to his chest, feeling the solid warmth of him through his t-shirt. When he makes a low sound in his throat, I move closer, climbing into his lap without breaking the kiss.

His hands grab my hips, pulling me flush against him, and I feel the unmistakable evidence of his growing interest pressing against me. The realization that he wants me this much sends a rush of heat through my entire body. His heart races against my palm as he leans in, and his tongue touches mine.

We're completely lost in each other when his hand slides under the hem of my sweater, his palm warm against the bare skin of my back. I arch into the touch, and he takes it as encouragement. His hand moves higher until his thumb brushes the edge of my bra.

"Stella," he breathes against my lips, and there's something desperate in the way he says my name.

I'm about to respond when his hand moves to cup my breast through the thin lace, and all coherent thought leaves my brain. I gasp against his mouth, and he takes advantage, kissing me deeper while his thumb traces my nipple through the fabric.

The sensation sends heat shooting straight through me, and I rock against him instinctively, using his hardness to ease the ache where I'm straddling him. He groans, and his other hand tangles in my hair to hold me exactly where he wants me.

My phone buzzes loudly on the coffee table, and the screen lights up with a notification.

We break apart, both breathing hard, staring at each other like we're not quite sure what just happened. His hand is still under my sweater, gripping my waist, my fingers are still fisted in his shirt, and the air between us is charged with electricity.

My phone buzzes again; the noise feels insistent.

"You should..." Brandon says, his voice rough, as he glances at the phone.

I reach for it with shaking hands, and we both see Mason's name on the screen. I swipe to read the message.

MASON

Great to see you tonight.

You up for some tennis this weekend?

The words feel like a splash of cold water. Reality crashes

back in, reminding me why we were doing this in the first place.

"That was..." I have no idea how to finish that sentence.

"Really good practice," Brandon says quietly, though his eyes are saying something entirely different.

I slide off his lap, immediately missing the warmth of his body against mine. "Thank you. For the lesson, I mean."

"Anytime," he says, his voice rough around the edges.

I stand on unsteady legs and smooth down my sweater, trying to process what just happened. "I should probably get some sleep."

"Yeah. Me, too."

But neither of us moves for a moment. We just look at each other like we're trying to memorize this feeling. Whatever just happened between us felt like a lot of things, but a lesson wasn't one of them.

"Goodnight, Brandon."

"Goodnight, sunshine."

As I walk to his bedroom, I can feel his eyes on me until I disappear through the door. I should respond to Mason, but instead, I plug in my phone and crawl into Brandon's bed, trying to figure out what kind of lesson that was.

twenty-three

. . .

Brandon

I STRAIGHTEN my tie one more time as I check my watch. Six o'clock exactly. The FlixPix premiere starts at seven, and with LA traffic, we need to leave in the next ten minutes if we want to make it on time.

Last night keeps replaying in my head like a movie. The way Stella felt in my arms on this very couch, how she tasted when I kissed her, and the soft sounds she made when my hands found their way under her sweater. If her phone hadn't gone off, who knows if we would have stopped. I've already had to take care of myself twice today just thinking about it.

I knock on the door to my bedroom, where she's been getting ready. "Stella? We need to head out soon."

"Almost ready!" she calls back. "Just need help with my zipper."

I push open the door and immediately forget how to breathe.

Stella is standing in front of my full-length mirror, dressed in a black dress. It's elegant and sophisticated, hitting just above her knee, with a neckline that shows just enough to be interesting without being obvious. Her hair is swept up in a way that shows off her neck, and she's wearing heels that make her legs look endless.

Christ. When did this happen? When did looking at Stella stop being casual and start making my mouth go dry? We've known each other for a few years now, but it's only been since she moved across the hall that we've gotten really close. And I've managed to keep things perfectly platonic this whole time. But standing here, watching her smooth down the fabric of that dress, all I can think about is not zipping her up and instead sliding that dress off of her.

"Wow," I manage. "You look—"

"Too much?" She turns toward me, suddenly uncertain, and the movement makes the dress shift in ways that definitely don't help my current situation. "I know it's more formal than usual, but I wanted to look the part tonight. Make a good impression for both of us."

This is ridiculous. A week ago, she was just Stella. Now I'm standing here trying not to imagine what she's wearing under that dress, and I feel like an absolute jackass for it.

"You look perfect," I say, my voice rougher than it should be. "Absolutely stunning."

I'm so fucked.

A flush creeps up her neck at the compliment, and I'm reminded of how she responded to my touch last night, how she arched into me when my hands—

"Zipper?" she says, turning around and pulling her hair to one side.

I step behind her, trying to ignore how the scent of her

perfume makes me want to lean closer, to press my lips to the spot where her neck curves into her shoulder. My fingers find the zipper at the base of her spine, and as I slowly pull it up, my knuckles brush against her skin with each inch.

"There," I say, stepping back before I do something stupid like kiss her neck. "Ready to go charm some industry executives?"

"Ready," she says, grabbing her clutch. "I'm pretty sure I can get us time with Helene tonight, and I really think this could be your in with her F1 series. She's building her stunt team now, and your racing background would be perfect."

The fact that she's thinking about my career, that she's using her industry connections to help me transition, makes a calm feeling spread through me. "Thank you. For bringing me tonight, for everything you're doing to help."

"That's what friends do for each other," she says, her eyes focused on everything around her but me.

Friends. The word hangs between us, loaded with implications we're both avoiding.

I clear my throat. "We should get your mother."

We cross the hall to Stella's apartment, where Caroline is waiting in the living room, looking elegant in a navy dress and pearls. She lights up when she sees us together.

"You look beautiful, Caroline," I say, offering her my arm.

"Thank you," she beams. "Stella, you're so lucky to have found such a gentleman."

As we head toward the elevator, Caroline glances back with a smile. "You two look perfect together."

Taking the cue, I catch Stella's hand and pull her closer.

"What are you—"

I cut her off by cupping her face and pressing my lips to hers.

It's meant to be quick, just a little show for her mother's benefit, but the moment our lips touch, the memory of last night comes rushing back. She melts into me immediately, her hands fisting in my jacket, and I have to force myself to pull away before we get carried away again.

"In case I forget to say it later, I really appreciate everything you are doing for me tonight." I give her one more quick kiss.

"For your mother," I murmur against her lips, though we both know it felt like much more than that.

"Right," she breathes, her cheeks flushed. "For Mama."

But as we follow Caroline into the elevator, I catch Stella touching her lips like she's trying to hold on to the feeling, and I wonder if any of this is an act for her anymore.

We make it to the theater with fifteen minutes to spare, just as the red carpet starts humming with camera flashes and shouted questions. Stella hooks her arm through mine as we approach the check-in table, her heels clicking in time with my steps.

She leans in to whisper something about how everyone suddenly turns into a red-carpet critic the second there's a velvet rope, and I bite back a laugh as we move through the line.

We say a quick hello to Sophia, Grant, Jess, and Lucas, introducing her mother to our friends before we enter the lobby space.

"There's Ava," Stella says, nodding toward the actress. Ava's hair is swept up in a glittery clip, and she's modeling an elegant black gown. I know Stella has been working hard to recalibrate her career. "And that's Helena talking to the producer near the step-and-repeat."

Helena Voss is younger than I expected, maybe late thirties, with short, dark hair and the no-nonsense vibe of someone who's allergic to incompetence. She's deep in conversation with a man in an expensive suit, gesturing animatedly about something.

"She grew up around Formula One," Stella explains quietly as we walk. "Her father was a pit crew chief for McLaren back in the day. This new series is apparently her love letter to that world."

We make our way through the reception area, and Stella expertly navigates all of us toward different groups, introducing her mother and me to people whose names I try to remember. Her hand finds mine naturally as we move through the crowd.

"Stella, darling!" Ava approaches us with a warm smile. "You look absolutely stunning. And Brandon, how lovely to see you again."

"Thank you, Ava. You look incredible yourself," Stella says, her voice shifting into that client-facing tone she uses so easily—warm, confident, just this side of admiring. "You remember my mother, Caroline Rhodes."

"Of course! Mrs. Rhodes, what a pleasure to see you again," Ava says, extending her hand graciously.

"Such a pleasure to see you again," Caroline says. "You look stunning this evening."

"You're very kind," Ava replies, then turns her attention

back to us. "And how are you two lovebirds doing? Still in that adorable honeymoon phase, I see."

Stella's hand grips my bicep as she leans in closer, and her other hand intertwines with mine like it's the most natural thing in the world. "We're wonderful, thank you."

"Brandon, remind me what you do again?" Ava asks. "I remember Stella mentioning you work in the industry."

"I'm a stuntman," I say.

Her eyebrows lift with genuine interest. "How exciting. Actual fire and flips or more of the precision driving and fight choreography side?"

"A little of everything," I say with a small laugh. "Lately, it's more wire work and fight scenes, but I've taken a flaming tackle or two."

Stella cuts in, her hand squeezing mine as she speaks. "He's being modest. He's currently working on this incredible action film, doing some really complex stunt sequences. But he's also looking to transition into coordination work. That's actually part of why we're here tonight."

I appreciate how she acknowledges my current work while positioning the transition as a strategic choice rather than a necessity. She makes it sound like I'm expanding my skill set rather than being forced to change direction because of physical limitations.

"Well, it's not hard to see why Stella's so proud of you," Ava says with a knowing smile. "You two have that lovely glow that new couples get when they're completely smitten with each other."

Caroline practically radiates approval beside us. "They

really do, don't they? I keep telling them how perfect they are together."

Ava's gaze flicks between us, taking in how Stella leans into me slightly, how my thumb traces across her knuckles without conscious thought. "Young love is such a beautiful thing. You can practically feel the chemistry between you two."

I see Stella's cheeks redden, but then notice her catch sight of someone across the room. "Ava, I want you to meet someone. Do you see that man by the bar in the red tie? That's Alex Chen. He's a creative executive at Wonderland Studios."

"Television?" Ava's nose wrinkles slightly.

"Comedy primarily, but he's working on some limited series and prestige projects. I think it would be good for you to meet him."

"Stella, dear, I'm a film actress. I don't really do television. This was a onetime thing. A favor, really, for Helena."

"I know," Stella says patiently, "but we're going to diversify your portfolio a bit. Trust me."

I watch as Stella expertly guides Ava toward Alex before making introductions with the kind of strategic thinking that reminds me why she's so good at her job. She's always three steps ahead, seeing opportunities that other people miss.

The lights flash, indicating it's time to take our seats. Stella reappears at my side, and Caroline joins us as we find our row.

"How did it go with Alex?" I ask as we find our seats.

"Good, I think. They're going to have coffee next week." She settles into her seat, automatically handing me her purse to hold while she adjusts her dress. "Oh, and I managed to get you a chance to say hi to Helena as soon as the show is over, but it will only be a three-minute window. Stay close and follow my lead."

"You're amazing," I tell her, and I mean it.

The lights dim, and we settle in just as the opening scene begins to roll. Ava's cameo comes about halfway through—just two lines and a loaded glance—but she nails it. And Helena? I didn't expect her direction to be this sharp. Every beat feels deliberate, like she's got something to prove and the talent to back it up.

As the credits roll and people begin filing out, Stella turns to her mother. "Mama, we're going to say a quick hello to someone for Brandon's work. We'll meet you by the exit in just a few minutes." Caroline nods approvingly, clearly pleased to see Stella supporting my career.

Stella grabs my hand and navigates us through the crowd toward Helena, who's surrounded by producers and network executives.

"Helena," Stella says warmly as we approach, "congratulations. The premiere episode was incredible—sharp, compelling, and that final scene? I actually gasped."

Helena's expression softens just slightly. "Appreciate that. We've pushed hard to get the tone just right."

"You nailed it," Stella says sincerely. Then, without missing a beat, she shifts gears. "I also wanted to introduce you to Brandon Grimaldi. He's one of the most talented stunt performers working right now, and with his racing background, I thought he might be a great resource for your F1 project."

Helena turns toward me and offers a firm handshake. "Nice to meet you."

"You, too," I reply. "I really enjoyed the show. Congratulations."

Her gaze is direct, with all her focus on me. "How long have you been in the business?"

"I've been doing stunt work for about fourteen years. I've worked on three racing films and understand both the practical and safety elements involved in automotive sequences."

"Interesting," she says, giving me a quick once-over like she's already plugging me into a shot list in her mind. "Stella, maybe you can set something up?"

"Of course," Stella says, already slipping into follow-up mode.

And just like that, Helena's pulled away by a swarm of producers. Stella looks over at me with that signature I-know-what-I'm-doing smile—and yeah, she absolutely does.

"That was perfect," she whispers as we move through the crowd toward the exit to find her mother.

But all I can think about is how perfect it feels to have her by my side.

twenty-four

* * *

Stella

BY THE TIME we get back to Brandon's apartment, it's past midnight, and my feet are killing me. Mama disappeared into my place across the hall with a satisfied smile and a comment about what a "lovely evening" it was, leaving Brandon and me alone in his living room.

I kick off my heels and immediately feel human again, while Brandon shrugs out of his suit jacket and loosens his tie. That's when I notice him rolling his left shoulder, trying to work out what looks like a painful knot.

"Your shoulder bothering you?" I ask.

"Just a little stiff," he says, but I can see the way he's favoring it. "The couch is comfy, but space is limited."

Guilt washes over me. He's been sleeping on that couch for a week because I took over his bedroom, and I never even thought about how uncomfortable it must be for him.

"Brandon, this is ridiculous," I say, heading toward the bedroom. "We're adults. We can share a bed without it being weird."

"Stella, you don't have to—"

"Yes, I do. I should have already offered." I turn back to face him with a pleading look. "I'm sorry I didn't think of it sooner."

He follows me into the bedroom. "It's fine, Stella, and I don't have to sleep in here if it makes you uncomfortable."

I turn to face him, trying to read the look on his face. Does he want to sleep in here?

"It doesn't."

"I promise to keep to my side of the bed," he says and starts to unbutton his shirt, which is my cue to leave.

"I'm going to rinse off this makeup and change," I say, grabbing my sleep clothes from the dresser. "Make yourself at home...in your own room...that I took over."

God, why am I so awkward?

When I emerge from the bathroom five minutes later in one of his old t-shirts and a pair of sleep shorts, Brandon is already in bed, propped up against the headboard with the covers pulled to his waist. And he's shirtless.

I try not to stare at the expanse of his chest, at the way his muscles shift as he reaches for his phone on the nightstand, but it's impossible. He's beautiful thanks to years of working out and building a body made for stunts. He's all golden skin and defined lines that almost look photoshopped.

"Much better," I say, hoping my voice sounds normal as I slide under the covers on my side of the bed.

The mattress dips slightly as I settle in, and I become hyperaware of how close we are. When I turn onto my side to face him, I catch him looking at me with an intensity that makes my skin feel warm.

His eyes travel from my face down to my chest, where it's obvious he's noticed I'm wearing one of his T-shirts. "You look good in my clothes," he says quietly.

"It's soft," I manage, though my heart is beating faster now.

"Thanks again for tonight," he says, his voice softer in the dim light. "Your mom seemed to have a good time."

"She loved every second of it. You're officially her favorite person." I smile. "Thank you for being so good to her. I know she can be a lot."

"She's not a lot. She just loves you."

We're facing each other, less than two feet apart, and the space between us feels charged with possibility. Every time he shifts, I catch another glimpse of his bare chest. Every time I move, his eyes seem to track the movement like he can't help himself.

"We should probably get some sleep," I whisper, though I make no move to turn away.

"Probably," he agrees, but his gaze drops to my lips for just a moment before meeting my eyes again.

Neither of us makes a move, and I think we both realize this is a dangerous temptation.

Finally, we each reach for our respective bedside lamps, and the room plunges into darkness as we click them off. I roll onto my other side, facing away from him, and pull the covers up to my chin, and I hear him do the same on his side of the bed. Now we're lying back to back in the dark, both of us perfectly still as we pretend this is perfectly normal.

But as I listen to his breathing gradually slow and deepen, I'm acutely aware of every inch of space between us, of how right it feels to have him beside me, of how much I want to close that distance.

It's the most peaceful I've felt in weeks, and I drift off to the sound of his steady breathing.

When I wake, the light from outside is spilling through the blinds.

And Brandon is holding me.

I'm on my side, facing him, and his arms are around my waist, pulling me close. Every inch of him is pressed against me. His chest, his hips, his thighs—all heat and muscle and sleep-warmed skin.

I should move. I should extract myself and go get ready for the day.

But I don't.

His body is solid beside me, grounding. And after everything that's happened this week between us, I can't bring myself to leave.

Then I feel it.

A slow, deliberate stroke of his thumb across my lower back. Barely there. But unmistakably real.

My heart lurches.

I stay still, eyes closed, breath held, like if I don't move, I won't shatter whatever spell this is. His breathing is shallow now, more conscious, and I know he's awake.

His thumb keeps moving in lazy circles, warmer now, bolder. I feel myself softening, melting into it, with the edges of my body blurring where his meets mine.

Then I feel his breath against my cheek.

And then his lips.

It's gentle at first. Careful. His mouth brushes mine like a question, and when I don't pull away—when I tilt forward instead—the kiss deepens, turning greedy, as our willpower unravels in one slide of lips and tongue.

He kisses me like I belong to him.

And I kiss him back like he's mine, too. This feels instinctive. Natural. Like I was always supposed to end up right here.

I shift carefully, sliding more on top of him. My thigh slips between his legs, and the sound he makes—a low, ragged groan—rattles through me like thunder.

His hands move to my hip, then lower, and his fingers dig into the curve of my ass, centering me on top of him like he's anchoring himself. I arch into him, chasing friction, and there it is—he's hard and hot and undeniable, pressing into me through his thin cotton briefs.

And God...*this*.

This doesn't feel like making out with someone I shouldn't. This feels like finding the thing I didn't know I needed.

His mouth trails from my lips to my jaw to the base of my throat, dragging open-mouthed kisses that leave me trembling. His teeth scrape my shoulder, peeking out from his shirt, and his palm covers my breast, his thumb circling over my nipple through the fabric.

The sensation makes my entire body jolt, and I gasp, clutching his side.

I've never felt this way before. No guy has ever made me feel this way.

It's not just physical. It's a full-body yes. My heart. My

skin. My mind, even as it flickers with a single warning: *He's your friend.*

But I don't stop. I don't think.

Not when Brandon's breathing my name like a secret. Not when his hand slides beneath my shirt and slides it off. Not when he caresses my bare skin, setting every nerve ending on fire.

I bite my lip, barely holding in the cry that rises when his thumb brushes my nipple again—this time with nothing between us.

He groans beneath me as his hips lift to meet mine, and my brain short-circuits. There's no space left for logic. No air for guilt.

Just heat. Need. Him.

"So fucking perfect," he whispers, his voice wrecked and reverent, and my whole body responds to the sound of it.

His palm continues to skim my breasts, his fingers touching skin that's never been touched by him before. And it's too much and not enough. My hips start moving instinctively, chasing every bit of pressure and drag I can get.

He feels big beneath me. I assumed he probably would be. He's tall, built, and his body is pure perfection. Why wouldn't every other part of him be the same? I rub my clit against his erection, rolling against it, seeking more. The fabric is soaked between my thighs. My body is alive in a way that feels dangerous—like, once this line is crossed, there's no turning back.

His fingers find the edge of my underwear, and his hand slips just beneath the waistband to palm my ass. I gasp, clinging to him.

I'm so close it's dizzying.

"I'm going to come," I whisper, my breath hot against his ear.

He groans, low and urgent, thrusting up to meet my movements, and it sends me over the edge.

It's not gentle. It's not quiet. It crashes through me like a storm as his name leaves my lips.

I bury my face in his neck as my body clenches around nothing and everything all at once.

His final thrusts bring me down and cause him to erupt, a sharp gasp against my skin. His hips rock with pleasure as he loses control, his release hot between us.

We collapse into stillness, bodies tangled, breath shallow, sweat cooling on flushed skin.

I can feel his heartbeat. Fast. Wild. Matching mine.

I don't open my eyes. I don't speak.

Because I know, the second I do, it'll be real.

I stay wrapped around him, my cheek against his chest, the scent of sex and his skin mixed with mine. Safe. Wanted. Completely undone.

And then—a bang on his front door.

"Stella? Brandon? Are you two in there?"

My mother's voice carries through the front door.

I push myself off him, my adrenaline surging, my heart pounding for a completely different reason now. My chest is bare, my shorts clinging and damp between my thighs, and my lips feel swollen and raw.

Holy shit. What just happened?

I can't think about it right now. Can't examine the way my body is still humming with satisfaction or the way

Brandon looked at me in those final moments. Can't acknowledge that everything between us has just changed completely.

I scramble off the bed before smoothing my hair, slipping his T-shirt back over my head with shaky fingers, and grabbing a pair of sweats I see on the chair in the corner of the room. Brandon's still catching his breath behind me, his eyes wide, stunned.

I don't look at him.

I can't.

Because if I do, I'll see everything we just did.

And everything we just risked.

twenty-five

Stella

"STAY HERE," I whisper.

Brandon nods, running both hands through his hair as he tries to catch his breath. He looks as stunned as I feel, his chest still rising and falling rapidly.

Another knock, more insistent this time.

"Coming, Mama!" I call out, doing a quick check in the hallway mirror. My hair is a disaster, and my lips are swollen, but there's nothing I can do about that now.

When I open the door, my mother is standing there, fully dressed, with her suitcase beside her, looking impeccable as always despite the early hour.

"Good morning, sweetheart," she says, taking in my rumpled appearance with obvious amusement. "I hope I'm not interrupting anything important."

Heat floods my cheeks. "Of course not. What's going on? Is everything okay?"

"Everything's perfect. I just wanted to say goodbye before my flight." She glances past me toward the bedroom hallway.

"I decided to catch an earlier one. I have a committee meeting this afternoon that I'd hate to miss."

"I can drive you to the airport," I offer automatically, though the thought of leaving right now feels impossible.

"Oh, no, darling. There's already a car waiting downstairs." She pulls me into a hug and whispers in my ear, "I didn't want to interrupt you lovebirds any more than necessary. You two looked so cozy last night."

If she only knew how cozy we'd been about thirty seconds ago.

"I had such a wonderful time," she continues. "Brandon is absolutely perfect for you, and seeing you two together just confirms what I already knew. You're meant for each other."

"Mama—"

"I'll call you when I land," she says and then kisses my cheek. "Give Brandon my love. And Stella? Don't overthink things. Sometimes, the best relationships are the ones that surprise you."

The way she says that, coupled with a knowing look, makes me wonder if she knows we were faking this whole relationship all along.

Before I can respond, she's heading to the elevator with her suitcase, leaving me standing in the doorway, trying to process what just happened.

I close the door, lean against it, and take a shaky breath. The apartment is quiet except for the sound of movement from the bedroom. A few moments later, Brandon emerges wearing basketball shorts and a gray t-shirt, his hair still messed up from my fingers, looking unfairly attractive despite, or maybe because of, how rumpled he is.

The sight of him makes my stomach flip as everything from the past half hour comes rushing back. The way he felt against me, the sounds he made, how right it felt until reality crashed in.

"She's gone?" he asks, his voice carefully neutral.

"Yeah. Caught an early flight." I fidget with the hem of his t-shirt, suddenly hyperaware that I'm still wearing it. "So, I guess that means I can move back into my place now. We can officially break up."

I try to make it sound light, joking, but it comes out flat and awkward instead.

"Right," Brandon says, shoving his hands in his pockets. "Back to normal."

"Back to normal," I echo, though nothing about this feels normal.

The silence stretches between us, filled with everything we're not saying. About what just happened. About how it felt. About what it means that we can barely look at each other now.

"I should probably get my things together." I gesture vaguely toward my stuff scattered around his apartment.

"Sure. Yeah. No rush."

But there is a rush because standing here looking freshly almost-fucked while he looks everywhere except at me is torture. I need space to think, to figure out what the hell just happened between us and why I feel despair deep in my bones when I think about going back to my empty apartment across the hall.

I start gathering my belongings: clothes I'd snuck into his dresser over the past few days, my toiletries, which had claimed a spot on his bathroom counter, and the work files I'd spread across his coffee table like I lived here. Each item I pack feels heavier than it should, like I'm dismantling something that was starting to feel permanent, even though it's only been less than a week. The toothbrush beside his, my sweater draped over his chair, the coffee mug I used every morning—all things that created an illusion of us that's hard to let go of.

Brandon helps wordlessly, handing me things and making space in the bag I'm using to carry everything back across the hall. Back to my own apartment, where everything will be exactly as I left it. Separate. The way it's supposed to be.

"I'll just..." I pause at his door, my bag heavy in my hands. "I'll catch up with you later."

Later. The word sits between us like a question neither of us knows how to answer. Later today? Later this week? Later, when we've both figured out how to pretend this never happened?

"Yeah," he says, opening the door for me. "Later."

I cross the hallway to my own apartment, and my key shakes slightly as I unlock the door. Inside, everything looks exactly the same as when I left it a week ago, but somehow, it feels different. Smaller. Emptier.

I drop my bag by the door and sink onto my couch, trying to make sense of what just happened. One week ago, we were just friends. Good friends who helped each other out and watched trashy TV on Thursday nights with our favorite takeout.

Now I have no idea what we are.

twenty-six

. . .

Brandon

MAN CHAT

JAKE

Welcome to the brotherhood, Brandon! About damn time we got you in here.

WYATT

Wait. Is the invite because of Stella? Or are we changing the rules?

LUCAS

Stella or no Stella, welcome to the fun.

GRANT

Saw you both at that FlixPix premiere last night – very cozy.

BRANDON

Thanks guys. But Stella and I are just friends.

JAKE

Friends? That's not how you looked at her at that wrap party.

BRANDON

I'm pretty sure I was looking at her like I always do.

WYATT

How were you looking at her?

JAKE

Anyway, apologies for the late add - but consider this your official invite to Manmorial Weekend.

JAKE

[Dropped pin]

LUCAS

Three days of golf, cigars, and questionable life choices.

GRANT

Speak for yourself. Some of us are reformed.

JAKE

Reformed my ass. You're bringing the poker chips.

BRANDON

It's an honor to be included.

WYATT

Stella can join the girls' weekend while you decompress with us. Win-win.

JAKE

Friday afternoon arrival, golf Saturday morning at Torrey Pines, deep sea fishing Saturday afternoon, poker and whiskey Saturday night. Sunday recovery and more golf.

LUCAS

Plus Jake's famous Sunday morning breakfast burritos that somehow cure every hangover known to man.

GRANT

Fair warning...Jake takes his golf very seriously. He'll be keeping score and talking trash.

JAKE

Damn right I will. Brandon, you play?

BRANDON

Some. Haven't had much time lately with work.

WYATT

Perfect excuse to get back into it. Nothing like ocean air and friendly competition.

LUCAS

By friendly he means Jake will crush your soul if you beat him.

JAKE

That's what makes it fun. So you in, Grimaldi?

BRANDON

Yeah, count me in. Sounds like exactly what I need.

GRANT

Excellent. Fair warning...no phones during poker. House rules.

JAKE

And no talking about work.

WYATT

Looking forward to having you there, man. It's about time.

BRANDON

Thanks for including me. Really.

LUCAS

Welcome to the club. Your liver may never forgive you.

twenty-seven

. . .

Brandon

I SHOULD PROBABLY STAY HOME and figure out what the hell just happened between Stella and me this morning. Instead, I'm driving to the studio lot like my apartment is on fire, needing to put distance between myself and the memory of how she felt in my arms before everything went sideways.

I grab two bottles of water to go with our lunch from the commissary and head outside to where Sophia's already claimed our usual picnic table under the big oak tree. The afternoon sun feels good on my shoulders, and I'm grateful for the day off.

"Please tell me you got the good sandwiches," Sophia says, looking up from her phone as I approach.

"Turkey club for you, Italian combo for me," I say, sliding the bag across the table. "And yes, I made sure they put extra avocado on yours."

"This is why you're my favorite," she says with a grin while unwrapping her lunch. "How's the morning been? You looked like you were moving pretty slow when I saw you walking across the lot earlier."

I rotate my shoulder experimentally. It's better than it was a month ago, but still not where it needs to be. "Just the usual bumps and bruises. Nothing a hot shower won't fix."

Sophia takes a bite of her sandwich and studies me with those sharp eyes that made her such a good child actress and an even better adult one. "So, how's everything else going? You seem different lately."

"Different how?"

"I don't know. Quieter, maybe? Less of that Brandon charm that usually has every woman on set asking me for your number."

I laugh despite myself. "Maybe I'm just getting old."

"You're thirty-two, not ninety-two." She pauses, then leans forward slightly. "Speaking of which, I heard through the grapevine that Marvel's doing another round of auditions for that new project. The one with all the practical stunts. Didn't you say you were interested in that?"

My stomach tightens. I've been dreading this conversation. "Yeah, I heard about it."

"And?"

I take a long drink of water, buying myself time. Sophia knows me too well to accept a casual brush-off, and honestly, I don't know why I'm keeping it a secret.

"I can't audition," I say finally.

"What do you mean you can't? Brandon, this is exactly the kind of opportunity you've been waiting for. Big budget, respected director, and they specifically want someone with your experience."

I set down my sandwich and look her directly in the eye. "I failed my last physical."

The words hang in the air between us. Sophia's expression shifts from confusion to concern.

"What do you mean you failed?"

"My shoulder. It's not healing like it should, and I can't pass the mobility tests they require." I try to keep my voice casual, but I can hear the frustration creeping in. "I'm doing physical therapy, and I go back for a retest in three months, but right now, I'd have to submit my current physical with any audition."

"Brandon." Her voice is soft now, the way it gets when she's worried. "Why didn't you tell me?"

"Because I didn't want you to worry. And because saying it out loud makes it real." I manage a smile. "Besides, it's not permanent. The PT is helping, and my therapist thinks I'll be cleared by the end of summer."

Sophia reaches across the table and squeezes my hand. "I can imagine how frustrated you must be."

It's not a question, and I don't try to deny it. "Yeah. I'm getting older, Soph. These injuries are taking longer to heal, and the recovery time between jobs keeps getting longer. I can't keep doing this forever."

"Does anyone else know?"

"Stella knows. She's actually been helping me think through some options. Career stuff."

"I'm glad you told her and she's helping you," Sophia says. "She's good at plotting out career options for people."

"She is. She's got some smart ideas on how I can stay involved in this world."

"What kind of options are you considering?"

I pick at my sandwich, grateful she's not pushing the injury topic. "Stunt coordination, obviously. Maybe choreography. I've been thinking about the teaching side, too. There are a lot of young stunt performers who could benefit from someone showing them the ropes properly."

"You'd be amazing at that," Sophia says immediately. "You basically taught me everything I know about on-set safety."

I smile at the memory. Sophia was fourteen when we first worked together on that spy show for the kids' network. Just a petite girl with dark brown hair, piercing blue eyes, and more talent than half the adults on set. I was doing easy stunts, playing the bumbling bad guy who always got caught, and she was this fierce little spy character who took down villains twice her size.

"You were a natural," I say. "You just needed someone to teach you how to do it without actually getting hurt."

"You did more than that." Her voice is serious now. "You looked out for me when a lot of people on sets didn't look out for kid actors. I don't know if I ever properly thanked you for that."

"You don't need to thank me. That's what good friends and self-nominated big brothers do."

She smiles at that. We've never talked about it explicitly, but somewhere along the way, that's what we've become: family.

"Well, let me return the favor," she says. "I can reach out to some of the coordinators I've worked with and get a sense of what opportunities might be out there. Unless Stella is doing that?"

"A little. Stella's been encouraging me to network more, actually. She says I need to start thinking of myself as a brand, not just a body for hire."

"That's really smart."

"She introduced me to Helena last night. I guess she has a new project starting soon at FlixPix, and Stella wanted me to be on her radar before she started hiring her crew."

"I can put in a good word, too. You'd be perfect on that project."

"Thanks, Soph."

"Speaking of Stella," Sophia says, settling back in her chair with that look she gets when she's about to dig into something. "How are things going with you two? Still fake dating and living together?"

"We're fine," I say, trying to keep my voice casual. "Her mom left this morning, so things should go back to normal."

"It was nice of you to step in as her fake boyfriend," she says, watching my face carefully.

"It wasn't a big deal. Just helped her out of a jam."

"Mmm." Sophia tilts her head. "Can I ask you something?"

I bite into my sandwich and take my time chewing. I know when I'm about to get grilled. "Sure."

When's the last time you went on a date?"

The question catches me off guard. "What does that have to do with anything?"

"Humor me."

I think back through the past few months. There was that

woman from the gym in March, but we never actually met up. Before that... "New Year's Eve, I think? That party at Wyatt's."

"Brandon, that was almost six months ago."

Has it really been that long? "I've been busy with work, physical therapy—"

"And Thursday nights with Stella," Sophia finishes gently. "Every Thursday night for how long now?"

"We're friends, Soph. Friends hang out."

"They do. But friends don't usually stop dating other people." She leans forward slightly. "I'm not judging. I'm just pointing out that maybe subconsciously, you've made yourself unavailable since she's moved in across the hall."

I want to argue, but something about the way she says it makes me pause. Have I been turning down opportunities? Making excuses not to go out with other women?

"She's interested in Mason anyway," I say finally.

"Is she?" Sophia says softly. "I'm not suggesting you run off and marry the girl, but seeing the two of you together last night and knowing how close the two of you have become, well, maybe there's a reason why it was so easy for you to fall into the role of boyfriend."

The truth is, it did feel natural. More than natural. It felt right in a way that scares me.

"I enjoyed it," I admit quietly. "More than I should have."

"And that terrifies you."

"Yeah. It does." I run a hand through my hair. "She's my friend, Soph. My really good friend. If I mess that up—"

"What if you don't mess it up? What if it's exactly what you both need?"

Before I can answer, my phone buzzes with a text from Jake sharing a packing list for Manmorial Weekend.

Sophia notices the notification. "You're going to La Jolla with the guys?"

"Finally got the coveted invite," I say, grateful for the subject change.

"Congratulations. Perhaps you'll get some perspective after some time away with them."

I nod, not trusting myself to respond. Because the thought of Stella as more than a friend both thrills and terrifies me in equal measure.

twenty-eight

. . .

Stella

BLAIR'S LIVING room has been transformed into the ultimate girls' night setup with blankets everywhere, wine glasses scattered across the coffee table, and enough takeout containers to feed a small army. But the real star of the show is baby Ruby, who's currently being passed around like the most precious item in existence.

"I can't get over how perfect she is," I say, cradling the tiny bundle against my chest. Ruby's fingers curl around mine, and something in my chest goes soft and warm. "Look at those little fingernails."

"She's got Wyatt's nose," Jess observes, leaning over to stroke Ruby's cheek. "But Blair's stubborn chin."

"She's going to be trouble," Sophia adds with a grin. "I can already tell."

Blair beams from her spot on the couch, looking tired but radiant. "She's been sleeping better this week, thank God. I was starting to forget what it felt like to be human."

"You're doing amazing," Natalie says warmly. "Single-handedly growing a human and then keeping it alive? That's superhero-level stuff."

After Ruby goes down for the night, we settle back with fresh glasses of wine.

"So," Jess says, leaning back into the couch and fixing me with that mischievous grin she gets when she's about to stir up trouble, "I think we all agree we want the update on your fake boyfriend."

"Which part?" I groan, already knowing where this is going. "When I blurted it out in a panic or when I had to move in with him for a week?"

"All of it!" Jess laughs. "But especially Brandon's face when you asked him to pretend to be madly in love with you. That man does not half-ass anything, so I can only imagine his reaction."

"He was surprisingly good at it," I admit, taking a large sip of wine. "Too good, actually."

Blair raises an eyebrow. "Too good how?"

"That's what I want to know," Natalie says, leaning forward with obvious interest. "Because you've been telling us for months how you two are 'just friends,' but something clearly shifted."

"Wait, back up," Sophia says. "How did things actually go with your mom? Did she buy it?"

"Completely. She absolutely adored him." I curl my legs up under me, getting comfortable for what I know is about to become a long story. "She kept going on about how perfect we were together, how he was such a gentleman, how I'd better not mess it up because good men like Brandon don't stay single forever."

"Smart woman," Jess says with a grin.

"But," I continue, and I can feel my cheeks warming, "some things didn't feel very fake."

"Finally!" Natalie exclaims. "I've been waiting for this part."

"There's nothing to wait for. We're just friends!" I protest.

"I told you not to jinx it. That shit creeps up on you when you least expect it," Jess says.

"What shit?" Blair observes with amusement.

"Feelings," Jess says, twisting her face in disgust, which is hilarious because those feelings are exactly what have her the happiest she's been in maybe ever.

"It's not my fault! The fake kissing was like a gateway drug. One minute, we're putting on a show for my mother; the next minute, we're making out on his couch like teenagers."

"Shut up!" Natalie jumps up to pour more wine into all of our glasses. "I'm going to need more specifics."

I bury my face in my hands. "It got complicated. Really complicated. By the end of the week, we were sharing a bed and waking up tangled together and..." I trail off, not sure how much detail to share.

"And?" Jess prompts, clearly not willing to let me off the hook.

"And let's just say we both needed cold showers afterward," I mumble through my fingers, "before my mother knocked on the door."

The room erupts in excited chatter as everyone talks at once.

"How was it?" Sophia asks with the kind of grin that suggests she already knows the answer.

"Mind blowing," I admit, then immediately want to take it back. "But nothing penetrating. We kept our clothes on. Mostly."

"Mostly?" Blair laughs. "Stella Rhodes, what exactly happened in that apartment?"

"A lot of heavy breathing and strategic positioning," I say, my face burning. "And hands under shirts. And some very creative use of fabric friction."

"Oh, my God," Jess gasps. "Did you dry hump Brandon Grimaldi?"

"Don't say it like that!" I protest, though that's exactly what happened. "It was intense. And confusing. And we've managed to avoid each other all week with dumb excuses about work being busy. And now everything's weird, and I don't know what any of it means."

"It means you have feelings for each other," Blair says matter-of-factly.

"But what if Brandon doesn't feel the same way? What if he was just caught up in the moment because we were playing house for a week?" The fear I've been carrying around all week finally comes spilling out. "What if I'm reading too much into everything?"

"Stella," Jess says, leaning forward with the kind of serious expression she usually reserves for investigative journalism, "I've known Brandon for years. I've watched him with women at parties, on dates, in casual hookup situations. He's charming, he's a gentleman, but he's also guarded. He doesn't let people get close."

"He's close with all of us," I point out.

"Not the same way he is with you," Blair says immediately.

The other women nod in agreement, and I look around at their faces, feeling like I'm missing something obvious.

"What do you mean?"

"I mean, he brings you actual meals when you're working late, not just coffee," Sophia says, as she counts off on her fingers. "He remembers which client meetings stress you out and texts you good luck before them. He automatically saves you the seat next to him at group dinners, and when you're talking, he turns his whole body toward you like nothing else in the room matters."

"Plus," Jess adds, "you two have your own language. All those inside jokes and looks across the room. And Stella, you fix his collar without thinking about it, you steal food off his plate like it's yours, and when he's telling a story, you finish his sentences."

"He has a key to your apartment," Blair mentions.

"Well, he's my neighbor. That's more of an emergency thing."

"He drops everything when you need help," Natalie adds.

"That's just friendship," I protest, but something in my chest is fluttering.

"No, honey," Blair says softly. "That's not just friendship. That's a man who's completely gone for someone and doesn't know how to say it."

"I don't know if you've noticed, Stella, but he's not dating," Sophia points out. "He hasn't been on a real date with anyone else since you two became close. And until your mother started laying on the pressure, neither of you have seemed interested in meeting other people anymore."

"That's not true. I went to trivia night with Mason. And I had asked Brandon to give me lessons on how to catch a guy's attention."

"Did Mason ever text you?" Natalie asks.

"He did."

"And?" Natalie pushes for more.

"It's complicated."

"Complicated how?" Sophia asks.

"Well," I say as I look around the room, all eyes on me. "His text came in while I was kissing Brandon. And it felt weird to reply. And then I may have told him I'd get back to him because I wasn't sure what was going on with Brandon."

"So, other than Mason, any other guys on the watch list?" Jess asks.

The room falls quiet for a moment, and the weight of realization settles over me.

"So, what do I do?" I finally ask, feeling lost, hopeful, and terrified all at once.

"You talk to him," Sophia says firmly. "When he gets back from his boys' weekend, you sit him down and have an honest conversation about what you both want."

"What if it ruins our friendship?"

"What if it doesn't?" Natalie counters. "What if it makes everything better?"

"Look," Jess says, reaching over to squeeze my hand. "You all but admitted that being fake-intimate with Brandon felt more real than anything you've ever experienced. That should tell you something."

As the evening winds down and we start cleaning up, I find myself thinking about Brandon somewhere in La Jolla with the guys. Wondering if he's thinking about me, too. Wondering if this time apart will give us both the clarity we need to figure out what comes next.

"You know what the best part is?" I say as we're gathering our purses to leave. "Even with all the confusion and weirdness, I miss him. It's been a few days, and I actually miss having him around."

"That's love, honey," Blair says softly. "When missing someone becomes as natural as breathing."

"I'm not ready to call it that," I say quickly.

"You don't have to call it anything," Sophia says, giving me a hug goodbye. "Just don't let fear make the decision for you."

As I Uber home to my empty apartment, their words echo in my head. One thing has become crystal clear tonight: whatever this thing is between Brandon and me, it's not going away. And maybe it's time to stop pretending it should.

twenty-nine

. . .

Brandon

I'VE BEEN to a lot of nice places in my life. Growing up in a family that owns luxury resorts all over has its perks. But Jake's Manmorial Weekend setup in La Jolla? This might actually top the penthouse suite at the Grimaldi Grande in Manhattan.

The house sits on the cliffs like it was carved out of the rock itself, all glass and white stone with views that stretch to infinity. I'm standing on the deck with a beer in my hand, watching the waves crash below as the sun creeps lower in the sky, and for the first time in months, my shoulder doesn't ache. Maybe it's the ocean air. Maybe it's the fact that I'm not hanging off a building or getting thrown through a fake window.

"Pretty incredible, right?" Jake appears beside me, carrying two fresh bottles. He swaps out my empty without me having to ask.

"This place is insane."

Jake laughs, but there's something tired in it. "Yeah, well,

Lauren got the house in Beverly Hills and half my assets. Figured I might as well blow what's left on something that actually makes me happy."

I study his profile as he stares out at the water. Jake's always been one of the good ones. He's loyal, grounded—the guy who sends reminders in the group chat and actually remembers your sister's name. He's sharp as hell in a boardroom and somehow still the guy who shows up with beer and snacks when someone's had a bad day.

Seeing him go through the divorce has been sobering, like watching someone who usually runs on pure optimism have to slow down and catch his breath. But even now, even with everything, there's still this quiet steadiness in him. Like he knows he'll be okay. Just needs a minute.

"You doing okay, man?" I ask.

He doesn't answer right away. Just takes a long sip of his beer, his eyes on the water.

"I thought I did everything right," he says finally. "Loved her. Backed her. Never missed a milestone, a red carpet, a lunch with her agent. I thought marriage was all about showing up and making sure she felt supported and loved, like she had it all."

He exhales through his nose, not bitter, just acknowledging the reality of the situation.

"Turns out, some people don't want a partner. They want to be bankrolled," he says.

I glance over, but he's already shaking his head, like he still can't believe how long it took him to see it. I stay quiet. Something tells me he's not done talking.

"Lauren wanted the ring, the house, the husband she could name-drop. She didn't want me. Just the access I had."

"She was—" I start, trying to tread lightly.

"Actually, a perfect casting option for *The Housewives of Beverly Hills,*" he finishes, smirking. "Season one, episode tragic."

I laugh, and so does he.

"But hey," Jake adds, lifting his beer toward mine. "I still believe in love. But this time, I'm holding out for someone who's there for me, loves me, supports me. Someone who's fine with takeout, a night in, and reruns on the TV."

That makes me think of Stella and our simple routines. How much I love the peace and comfort I feel with her. And the shame I feel about avoiding her all week because I didn't know how to tell her I want to be her real boyfriend.

He leans his arm on the railing, his gaze fixed on the ocean. "That's the good stuff, man."

And I don't disagree.

Before I can respond, Lucas calls from inside. "Jake! Your boy Austin's on the news!"

We head back into the main room, where Jess's brother, Austin Lexington, is giving an interview on ESPN, talking about his recovery from Tommy John surgery. He looks good, confident—the kind of confidence that comes from knowing you're about to get back to doing what you were born to do.

"He'll be here tomorrow," Lucas says. "Flying in after his PT session."

"Still can't believe Jess's little brother is Austin fucking Lexington," Jake says from the kitchen island, where he's now assembling what looks like the world's most elaborate charcuterie board. "I've been watching him pitch since he played for USC."

"Wait until you meet him," Lucas says with a grin. "Kid's exactly like Jess but with a ninety-seven-mile-per-hour fastball and significantly less terrifying opinions about your life choices."

Alex Chen, the studio executive from Wonderland whom I met at Lucas's dinner party last year, looks up from the poker game where he's been quietly demolishing Grant and Wyatt. "Speaking of life choices, Grimaldi, when are you going to stop throwing yourself off buildings for a living?"

It's a fair question. One I've been asking myself more and more lately. "Maybe sooner than I planned."

"Your shoulder still bugging you?" Jake asks with genuine concern.

I roll my shoulder experimentally. It's better than it was a month ago, but not the same. Probably never will be.

"Among other things," I admit. "The stunt work's been good to me, but I don't know how much longer I can keep crashing through windows and getting lit on fire before my body calls it quits."

Grant leans forward, his eyebrows raised. "You ever think about what's next? I mean, if you're serious about shifting gears, I know people. I'm happy to make a few introductions."

"Same here," Wyatt adds, sipping his drink. "You've got the chops. If you wanted something more behind the scenes —coordinating, consulting—there's plenty of work that won't land you in physical therapy."

I nod, genuinely touched. "Appreciate that."

Grant grins. "Besides, you'll never get domesticated if you

keep risking your life for a paycheck. Women love a man who comes home in one piece."

"Speaking of women," Alex says with a knowing smile, "I know the whole thing with Stella was supposed to be fake, but it looked anything but fake at that FlixPix premiere. What's actually going on there?"

I feel my chest tighten. "Nothing's going on. We're just friends. Her mom left last week, so the whole fake-boyfriend thing is over."

"Come on," Lucas says, grinning. "I saw you two at that premiere. If that was acting, you deserve an Oscar."

"Yeah," Grant adds. "I've seen you with actual girlfriends, and you looked less invested in them than you did with Stella that night."

Alex nods. "The way you two moved together, the little touches, how you kept checking to make sure she was comfortable? That wasn't acting, man."

The guys exchange looks, and I realize they're not buying my deflection for a second.

"Look," I say, running a hand through my hair, "maybe there were some moments. But it was just the situation. Playing house for a week, you know? Things got a little blurred."

"Blurred how?" Wyatt asks, and there's something knowing in his tone that suggests the wives have been talking.

"It doesn't matter," I say quickly. "She's not interested in anything more than friendship."

"Are you kidding?" Lucas laughs. "Brandon, the woman looks at you like you hung the moon. Whatever you're worried about, it shouldn't be whether she's interested."

"You don't know that."

"We all know that," Wyatt says.

"So," Jake says quietly, "what are you going to do about it? Because, from where I'm sitting, you both want the same thing, but you're too scared to say it."

"It's complicated," I say finally.

"The best relationships usually are," Jake says quietly.

I think about Stella, about how she felt in my arms that morning, about how right it felt to wake up with her tangled around me. About how empty my apartment has felt since she moved back across the hall.

Before I can respond, my phone buzzes with a text notification. For a split second, I hope it's Stella, but it's just my sister Nina asking about my weekend.

The guys have moved on to other topics, but their words echo in my head.

Maybe they're right. Maybe it's time to stop pretending that what happened between Stella and me was just acting. Maybe it's time to figure out what we actually are when we're not performing for her mother.

"Enough relationship therapy," Jake says, clapping his hands together. "Grimaldi, I need to know about the fight choreography in that *Roadhouse* remake. That bar scene where you take on four guys at once? How the hell did you make that look so real?"

Now this, I can talk about. I spend the next twenty minutes breaking down the choreography, explaining how we used the environment, how each hit was calculated for maximum visual impact with minimum actual damage. Jake's eating it up, asking technical questions that prove he knows what he's talking about.

But even as I explain the technical details, part of my mind is still on Stella. On what I'm going to say to her when I get back. On whether I'm brave enough to risk our friendship for the chance at something more.

Because, sitting here with these guys, all of whom have found their people and built lives worth living, I'm starting to realize that maybe what I want isn't just someone to pass time with. Maybe I want what they have. Partnership. Someone who's there for the good days and the bad. Someone who makes everything better just by existing.

Maybe I want Stella.

thirty

. . .

Stella

I'M FUMBLING with my keys outside my apartment door when I hear the elevator ding behind me. I turn to see Brandon stepping out, looking tanned and relaxed. He's carrying a weekend bag and wearing a soft gray t-shirt that makes his eyes look even more golden than usual.

His face lights up when he sees me. "Hey. Perfect timing."

"Hey, yourself." I can't help but smile back. "How was Manmorial Weekend?"

"Amazing. Really amazing." He sets down his bag to fish for his own keys. "The house was incredible, the golf was terrible, and I think I consumed my body weight in whiskey."

"I'm so happy for you," I say, and I mean it completely. "You've been wanting that invitation forever."

"Yeah, it felt good to finally be included." He pauses, studying my face. "How was your weekend? Did the girls spoil you properly?"

"They did. Blair's baby is absolutely perfect, and we may have consumed our own body weight in wine and gossip."

We're both standing in the hallway now, keys in hand, but neither of us is making a move toward our respective doors. The air between us feels charged, like there's something important hovering just beneath the surface of this casual conversation.

"Stella, I—"

"Can we talk?" I blurt out at the same time.

We both laugh, and the tension breaks slightly.

"Your place or mine?" he asks, but he's already unlocking his door.

"Yours," I say, following him.

The click of him sliding the lock closed sounds louder than it should, like it seals us off from the rest of the world. The space feels different somehow.

As he turns to face me, a question is already forming in his eyes.

But I don't want him to say anything. If he does, I'll lose my nerve, and I've already spent too many nights wondering what this would feel like. Wondering if the tension between us is as unbearable for him as it is for me. The girls' encouragement, the realization that I've been thinking about him as a possibility, the way my heart jumped when I saw him in the hallway—it all churns in my chest.

And I realize I'm done pretending.

I close the distance and kiss him, sure this time, greedy for the taste of him, my hands fisting in his shirt like I'm afraid he might vanish if I don't hold on.

He reacts instantly, like I've touched a match to something inside him. His arms wrap around me, pulling me flush against him, and the rough sound he makes hits me low in my stomach.

"I want to stop pretending I don't want you," I whisper against his mouth as my forehead brushes his. "I'm so tired of pretending."

His gaze drops to my lips, then back to my eyes, like he's making sure I mean it. "Are you sure? Because, once we cross this line, I don't think I can go back to just being your friend."

"I don't want to go back."

That's all the permission he needs. He surges forward, and his mouth crashes onto mine with a hunger that pulls the breath from my lungs. His hands slide into my hair, his fingers curling tight as if he can't stand the thought of me pulling away. The kiss is deep and consuming, and his tongue teases mine until my knees threaten to give out.

"God, Stella," he groans against my lips. "You taste so fucking good. So sweet and warm." His nose brushes mine as his mouth moves to my cheek, then lower to my jaw. "I can't stop thinking about you. About the way you felt pressed against me that night—your body rubbing against mine, soft and perfect, like you were made to fit there."

He drags his lips along my throat, inhaling deeply, like he's memorizing me. "Your skin..." His lips trail over my jaw, my ear. "Your mouth, your lips. I've been dying to have them on me again." His mouth claims mine again, harder this time.

His admission sends electricity through my entire body. I reach for the hem of his shirt, needing to feel his skin against mine, and gently peel it up over his head, careful with his shoulder. My hands explore the planes of his chest, the muscles that flex under my touch, the way his breathing hitches when my fingers trace the line of his collarbone.

"You're so beautiful," I murmur, and he makes a sound like I've undone him completely.

His hands find the zipper of my dress, and he pauses, his eyes meeting mine. "Tell me you want this."

"I want this, Brandon. I want you."

The zipper slides down slowly, deliberately, and a shiver races over my skin as the fabric falls away. For a heartbeat, I forget how to breathe. His gaze roams over me, almost worshipful, but there's heat there, too, a hunger that makes me feel unsteady.

"You're perfect," he says, his voice rough and certain, like he's stating a fact. "Absolutely perfect."

I should laugh it off, make some self-deprecating joke the way I always do when someone gets too close, but I can't. Not with the way he's looking at me. His eyes capture mine, and they tell me everything I've been hoping to know: that he's been waiting for this, not for days or weeks, but maybe longer, maybe his whole life.

He lifts me easily. My legs instinctively wrap around his waist, and the press of his body against mine steals my breath. God, he's hard. The contact is dizzying, electric, sending a pulse of heat straight between my thighs. I've been kissed before, touched before, even slept with men before, but nothing has ever felt like this.

He carries me to the bedroom and sets me down on his bed. His hands are sure but tender, mapping the slope of my shoulders, the curve of my waist, and the delicate skin below my ear. I gasp, arching toward him before I can stop myself.

"Tell me what you like," he murmurs as his lips brush my throat. "Tell me what you want."

I hesitate, my cheeks warming. "I don't know. I've never... With the other guys, it was never—"

"Never what, baby?"

I swallow, and the words barely make it past my lips. "Never where I felt like I might come apart just from being touched."

Something flickers in his eyes, heat layered over a kind of determination that makes my pulse spike. He bends to that spot under my ear again, and his teeth graze my skin just enough to make me whimper. "We're going to figure out exactly what you like," he promises, and the confidence in his voice curls low in my stomach. "And I'm going to make you come apart so many times you lose count."

The boldness of it should make me blush. Instead, it sends a flood of heat through me so intense I have to bite back a moan. Maybe I should be embarrassed by how little I know, how little I've experienced, but with him, I'm not.

His experience doesn't intimidate me. In fact, it feels like an anchor, something steady I can trust. He's confident and deliberate, like making me feel good is the only thing on his mind. And with every touch, I let go of the need to overthink or to perform. I just want to feel.

When his fingers move to the clasp of my bra, I don't hesitate. I want his hands on me. I want to know what it's like to be wanted like this. The straps slide from my shoulders, the last barrier falling away, and his breath catches.

"Christ, Stella," he murmurs as his hands cup my breasts with a reverence that makes my throat tighten. His thumbs brush over my nipples, and the sensation is so sharp, so consuming, I can't hold back the raw sound that escapes me.

"Do that again," I gasp, and he does, rolling and teasing until I'm trembling in his hands, my every nerve ending lit up.

"Lie down for me," he says, and I do, watching as he takes a moment to just look at me spread out on his bed. "I've dreamed about this," he admits. "About how you'd look, how you'd taste, how you'd sound, how I could make you feel good."

"Brandon, please."

He joins me on the bed, and his mouth finds mine again before trailing down my body with the kind of attention I've never experienced. When he reaches my breasts, he takes his time, alternating between gentle kisses and an intensity that has me gasping his name.

"So responsive," he murmurs against my skin. "I love the sounds you make."

His hands continue their exploration, mapping every curve and hollow like he wants to memorize me. When he reaches the edge of my underwear, he pauses again and looks up at me.

"Can I taste you?"

The question, asked so directly, makes me blush. I nod, not trusting my voice. He hooks his fingers in the lace and slides it down my legs with agonizing slowness.

"God, you're gorgeous," he says, settling between my thighs. "All of you."

The first touch of his mouth is gentle, exploratory, and I

nearly come off the bed. No one has ever touched me like this, with such obvious pleasure in giving pleasure.

"Brandon," I gasp as my hands fist in his hair.

"I know, baby. Let me take care of you."

He works me with his tongue, lips, and the gentle pressure of his fingers until I'm completely lost, my body moving against his mouth as tension builds higher and higher. When his fingers slide inside me, curling in just the right way while his tongue circles that perfect spot, I shatter completely.

"That's it," he encourages, working me through the waves of sensation. "So beautiful when you let go."

When I finally come back to myself, he's pressing soft kisses to my inner thighs, my hipbones, the sensitive skin of my stomach, giving me time to recover.

"I need you," I manage, my voice breaking as I reach for him. "Please, Brandon. I need you inside me."

He stills, his weight braced above me, his eyes locked on mine. For a long heartbeat, neither of us moves. It's like the air changes, and I know we're both thinking the same thing. Once we do this, we can't go back. But looking at him now, feeling the heat of his body, I know I wouldn't want to. No matter what happens tomorrow, next week, or next year, this will be worth it.

He lowers his forehead to mine, and our breaths mingle. His gaze is so deep that it feels like he's seeing all the pieces of me I usually keep hidden. "Are you sure?" he asks, his voice low, almost reverent.

"I've never been more sure of anything."

He reaches for his nightstand, fumbling for a condom, and I help him roll it on with shaking hands. When he settles between my thighs, the head of him pressing against me, we both go still.

"Look at me," he says softly, and I do. Our eyes lock as he pushes inside me slowly, giving me time to adjust. The stretch is perfect, the fullness everything I didn't know I was missing.

"Okay?" he asks, his voice strained with the effort of holding still.

"More than okay. Keep going."

He starts agonizingly slow, with each thrust deliberate and deep, like he's learning me from the inside out. And it's nothing like I imagined. I thought being with him would be all fire and speed, cocky skill and showmanship. And yes, there's that, but there's also something I didn't expect. The way his hand cradles my jaw between kisses, the way his thumb sweeps over my cheek as if he needs the connection as much as I do.

Every movement is a study in control, like he's savoring every inch, every sound I make, every sharp breath and soft moan. Then his control slips—just a fraction at first—with his hips driving harder, deeper, and his mouth finding mine in a kiss that's all heat and teeth. That shift from tender to feral sends a thrill through me so intense that I arch against him, chasing more.

"You feel incredible," he breathes, the words ragged between thrusts. "Perfect. Like you were made for me."

The way he says it, like it's not just sex, like it's a truth he's been carrying, pushes me closer to the edge. And when his hand slides between us, finding exactly where I need him, the combination is too much. Pleasure rips through me, and my nails dig into his shoulders as I cry out his name.

"Stella..." My name on his lips is a groan, a prayer, and the sound of it makes every nerve ending spark. I'm still riding the aftershocks, my body pulsing around him, and it's like that's all it takes to make his control snap. His pace falters, then turns urgent, almost rough, with each thrust deeper than the last.

His eyes lock on mine, raw and unguarded, and I can see the moment he can't hold back any longer. I cup his face, needing him close, and he drives into me one last time before shattering, with my name spilling from his lips like it's the only word he's ever known.

When he finally stills, his chest heaving, he stays close, resting his forehead against mine. As both of us breathe in the same ragged rhythm, I realize I've just let him see every part of me, and I don't regret a single second.

"Stay," he murmurs against my hair. "Stay with me tonight."

"Yes," I whisper before pressing a kiss to his chest. "Yes, I'll stay."

thirty-one

. . .

Brandon

I WAKE up to sunlight streaming through my bedroom windows and the most incredible sensation I've ever experienced—Stella Rhodes curled against my chest like she belongs there. Her blonde hair spills across my pillow, catching the morning light, and her breathing is soft and even against my skin. For a moment, I don't move, don't even breathe, terrified that any sudden motion might shatter whatever magic happened between us last night.

But then she stirs, her body stretching languidly against mine, and I remember. This is real. She's here. She chose me.

"Morning, beautiful," I say, my voice rough with sleep.

She tilts her head up to look at me, and Christ, she's gorgeous. Her blue eyes are soft and unfocused, her lips slightly swollen from my kisses, her cheeks flushed pink.

"Morning." She stretches against me again, deliberately this time, and my control evaporates as her body moves against mine. "How are you feeling?"

"Like the luckiest man alive," I say simply before pressing a kiss to her forehead. It's the truth. After years of keeping things casual, of never letting anyone get too close, I finally understand what all the fuss is about. This feeling of rightness, of completion, of finding the person who makes everything else make sense.

"How are you feeling?" I ask, though part of me is terrified of the answer. What if she regrets this? What if the harsh light of morning makes her realize she's made a mistake?

"Like I finally understand what all the fuss is about," she admits, and her words echo my thoughts so perfectly that I have to laugh.

"Good," I say, rolling her beneath me and enjoying the way her breath catches. "Because I plan on showing you a lot more of what the fuss is about."

This time, we go slow. Whereas last night was desperate and consuming, this morning we explore each other with a reverence that feels sacred. I map every inch of her skin with my hands and mouth, learning what makes her gasp, what makes her arch against me, what makes her whisper my name like a prayer.

When I reach for a condom, she watches me with heavy-lidded eyes that make my hands shake slightly as I tear open the wrapper. The trust in her gaze, the way she looks at me like I'm everything she's ever wanted, nearly undoes me.

When I slide inside her, slow and deliberate, we both go still. The sensation of being with her like this is overwhelming, and the way she looks at me—like I'm her whole world—makes my chest tight with emotion I don't have words for.

"Brandon," she whispers, her hands fisting in my hair, and I know I'll never get tired of hearing my name on her lips like that.

"I've got you."

We find a rhythm that's unhurried and perfect, our bodies moving together like we've been doing this for years instead of hours. When she comes apart beneath me, her back arching and my name spilling from her lips, I follow her over the edge, burying my face in her neck and breathing her in.

Afterwards, we lie tangled together in the morning light, her head on my chest, both of us trying to process what this means. But eventually, reality intrudes—I have a meeting that could change everything for my career, and Stella has clients to call. We move around each other in the bathroom and kitchen with a new kind of intimacy, stealing kisses while I shave and she makes coffee, like we're testing out what this domestic thing might feel like.

"Good luck today," she whispers against my lips as I'm heading out the door. "You're going to be amazing."

"Can I see you later?"

"Definitely."

An hour later, I'm across town, trying to focus on the biggest opportunity of my professional life.

The FlixPix offices in Culver City are sleek and modern in that way that screams, "We have money, and we're not afraid to spend it!" I'm sitting in a conference room on the fifth floor, waiting for Helena Voss, trying not to feel like I'm interviewing for my future. Which, let's be honest, I probably am.

Helena sweeps in five minutes later, all energy and purpose, moving with the kind of intensity that makes you understand how she sold a high-budget racing series to a streaming platform.

"Brandon, thank you for coming in," she says, settling across from me with a stack of scripts and what looks like a tablet full of storyboards. "I'll be honest, when I heard you were interested in transitioning to coordination work, I was intrigued. Your reputation precedes you."

"Good things, I hope."

"The best things. I've seen your work on the *Roadhouse* remake, the Wonderland Studios films, that insane car chase sequence in *Fast & Furious*. You have an eye for making action feel real without sacrificing safety." She leans forward. "Tell me why you want to make the switch."

This is the question I've been preparing for, but somehow, it still catches me off guard. How do you explain that your body is starting to betray you without sounding like damaged goods? How do you admit that you're tired of being the guy who gets thrown through windows instead of the guy who figures out how to make it look good?

"I love this business," I say, and the honesty in my voice surprises me. "I've been doing stunts for fourteen years, and I still get excited every morning when I show up to set. But as I get older, I can feel the difference. Recovery takes longer. The moves that used to be second nature require more thought, more preparation."

Helena nods, no judgment in her expression.

"I want to stay in this world for as long as possible," I continue. "And coordination lets me use everything I've learned while building something bigger than just my own performance. I want to create sequences that make audiences forget they're watching a movie. I want to mentor younger stunt performers the way the coordinators I worked with mentored me."

"That's exactly what I want to hear," Helena says. "Let me tell you about *Pace*."

She turns her tablet toward me, showing concept art of sleek Formula One cars racing through Monaco, Silverstone, and other tracks I recognize from watching races with my dad.

"It's the story of the first woman to break into Formula One as a driver," she explains. "Not just as a novelty or a publicity stunt, but as a real contender for the championship. We're following her rookie season as she deals with sexism, rivalries, media pressure, and the constant threat of death that comes with driving two hundred miles per hour."

The concept art is stunning: high-speed chases through narrow European streets, crashes that look devastating but controlled, close-ups of drivers' faces that capture the terror and exhilaration of the sport.

"The network is giving us a budget that would make most feature films jealous," Helena continues. "But they want everything to look and feel completely authentic. No CGI shortcuts, no AI, no obvious stunt doubles. When our lead character is racing, the audience needs to believe she's actually behind that wheel."

"That's ambitious," I say, studying the storyboards. "And expensive."

"Very. Which is why I need someone who can design

sequences that look incredible while keeping everyone alive." She flips to a particular scene. "This is the one I've been struggling with. It's the climax of episode six. Our protagonist is racing at Monaco, and there's a multi-car accident that she has to navigate while going full speed."

I look at the storyboard, and immediately I can see the problems. The angles are wrong, the timing is impossible, and there's no way to make it safe for real drivers.

"May I?" I gesture to her tablet.

She slides it over, and I start sketching rough modifications on the digital storyboard. "You're thinking about this like a traditional car race, but Formula One is different. The cars are lower, faster, more responsive. We had a similar setup on a commercial I did with the Bobby Ore team last year—tight angles, low rigs, full-speed run through a closed course in Burbank. If you don't plan for sight lines and trajectory, someone's going to get clipped. Instead of trying to stage the whole accident in one shot, you break it into pieces."

I draw quick lines showing different camera angles. "You start with the wide establishing shot of the accident beginning. Then you cut to interior shots of our lead seeing it develop. Then extreme close-ups of wheels, debris, sparks. By the time you cut back to the wide shot of her navigating through the wreckage, the audience will be so invested they won't question how she managed it."

Helena watches as I work, occasionally asking questions about sight lines and safety protocols. This is what I love about coordination work. It's like solving a three-dimensional puzzle where every piece has to serve both the story and the people performing it.

"You use stunt drivers for the wide shots," I continue, "but your lead actress only needs to be in the car for the close-ups and reaction shots. You can shoot those at thirty miles per hour and make them look like two hundred with the right camerawork and sound design."

"Brilliant," Helena says, and she sounds like she means it. "That's exactly the kind of thinking I need on this project."

We spend another twenty minutes going through other scenes, and I find myself getting more excited than I've been about work in months. This isn't just about making things look cool. It's about telling a story that matters, about bringing a character to life in a way that's never been done before.

"This is exactly the kind of vision I need for this project," Helena says as we wrap up. "I'm really impressed, Brandon. You'll definitely be hearing from me soon. I need to work through some formalities on my end, but..." She pauses, and there's something that feels like a promise in her smile. "Let's just say I think this could be the beginning of a very exciting partnership."

"I hope so," I say, and I mean it more than I've meant anything in a long time.

"I heard through the grapevine that you and Stella are together now," Helena says with a knowing smile. "She's lovely, by the way. Very sharp."

"We're just friends," I say automatically, then immediately feel like an ass for it. It's not that I want to hide what happened between us, far from it. But Stella and I haven't even talked about what crossing the friendship line means, and the last thing I want is for her to hear through the Hollywood rumor mill that I'm telling people we're together before we've figured out what we actually are. She deserves better than that. We both do.

"Really?" Helena raises an eyebrow. "Could have fooled me at that premiere. You two had some serious chemistry."

"She's a good friend," I repeat, hating how the words taste like a lie.

"My assistant will send you some additional materials to review. Keep your schedule flexible for the next few weeks."

I shake Helena's hand, thank her again, and walk out of the building feeling ten feet taller. It's the kind of meeting that makes all the years of bruises and uncertainty feel like momentum instead of survival. My phone buzzes as I cross the street toward my car.

Stella.

The second I see her name, I'm already smiling. Of course she's the first person I want to tell.

"Hey, sunshine."

"Tell me everything," she says immediately, her voice full of that warm, giddy energy that always makes things feel bigger, better. "How did it go? Was she scary? Did you crush it?"

I laugh, still high from the adrenaline. "Helena was intense in the best way. Straight to the point, no fluff. But yeah, I think I crushed it. She asked about my background, my experience with racing films. Said to keep my schedule open."

"Brandon, that's huge," she says, and I can *hear* the smile in her voice. "I'm so proud of you."

The words land deeper than she probably knows.

"Thanks. It felt good. Like...maybe this is the next chapter, you know?"

"It is," she says softly. "It totally is. You've worked your ass off. You deserve every bit of this."

Part of me hopes that she's talking about more than my career.

thirty-two

Stella

I'M TRYING to listen to Brandon tell me about his meeting with Helena, I really am, but it's hard to focus when his lips wrap around that fork like I imagine it would look wrapped around my breast and his tongue keeps sweeping out to lick food off said fork just like he might with my nipple.

I don't think I've ever been this horny in my life. We're sitting at his kitchen island with takeout containers between us, attempting to have a normal conversation, but every casual touch makes my skin buzz with awareness.

"She said to keep my schedule open," he says, his eyes bright with excitement. "Hopefully, I'll hear something by the end of the week."

"That's incredible," I manage, though my voice comes out breathier than intended because his free hand just settled on my thigh under the counter. "You deserve this, Brandon. You're going to be amazing."

"I couldn't have done it without you pushing me to take the leap." His fingers tighten slightly on my leg. "You're so smart and talented. Blair is lucky she found you. You're going to really change this industry."

His words make my heart skip. I love what I do, but I love it even more when people can see my value. I should say thank you, or maybe tell him how proud of him I am, but all I can think about is how his hands feel on my body. And how I can't get enough of this gorgeous man in front of me.

"We should celebrate," I say, then immediately feel my cheeks warm at how that came out.

"What did you have in mind?" He says with a knowing look on his face.

Before I can answer, he's pulling me off my stool and against his chest, and then we're kissing with the desperate hunger of people who've been denied something they didn't know they wanted. The takeout is forgotten as his hands slide down to cup my ass, and he lifts me onto the counter.

"We should probably talk about this," I murmur against his lips, even as my legs wrap around his waist. "Figure out what we're doing."

"Mmm," he agrees as his mouth moves to my neck. "Definitely. Very important conversation."

"It can probably wait—Oh, God, yes, right there—we'll figure this out tomorrow."

"Tomorrow," he says, his teeth grazing my pulse point. "We'll figure it all out tomorrow."

Tomorrow sounds perfect because, right now, his hands are pushing my dress up my thighs and I can't remember why talking seemed important. I pull his shirt over his head, marveling at how different it feels to touch him when I'm allowed to want him. When he's mine to explore.

He lifts me off the counter, with my legs still wrapped around him, and carries me to the bedroom. The confidence in his movements, the way he handles my weight like I'm nothing, sends sparks up my spine.

"I want to taste you," he says as he sets me down beside his bed. "I've been thinking about it all day."

My breath catches. "You have?"

"You taste so fucking delicious." His hands find the zipper of my dress. "It'll never be enough."

The dress pools at my feet, leaving me in just my bra and underwear. Brandon's gaze travels over me for a moment before he strips me bare.

"You're so beautiful," he breathes.

He guides me back onto the bed, following me down with kisses that make my toes curl. When his mouth finds my breast, I arch up into him, begging for more.

His hands and mouth worship me with a patience I've never experienced before. Every kiss is deliberate, every touch focused on my pleasure rather than rushing toward some goal. He trails kisses down my stomach. Then he settles between my thighs, and I have to close my eyes at the intensity of his gaze.

"Spread those legs, sunshine," he says with a gruff determination.

The first touch of his tongue makes me cry out, and my back arches off the bed. He's gentle but thorough, learning what makes me gasp, what makes me grip the sheets. And in no time, between his fingers, lips, and tongue, all fighting for my pleasure, my insides begin to clench.

"I'm close," I gasp, surprising myself.

"Good. Let go for me."

When the orgasm hits, it's like nothing I've ever felt. Wave after wave of pleasure crashes over me, and Brandon works me through all of it, his mouth never stopping until I'm boneless and shaking.

"That was..." I start, but I can't find words.

"I need to be inside you now," he says with a hint of urgency as he presses a kiss to my inner thigh.

"Wait," I tell him as he moves up my body, kissing me softly. "I want to do that for you."

"You don't have to—"

"I want to." I push against his chest until he's on his back. "But I should probably warn you, I'm not very experienced with that."

His eyes soften. "We'll go slow."

I work his pants off with hands that shake slightly from nerves and anticipation. When he's left in just his boxer briefs, I take a moment to appreciate him. He's beautiful, all lean muscle and golden skin. I admire the defined ridges of his abs, the curve of his biceps, and the broad expanse of his chest. His body is a work of art.

My eyes travel lower, and I see how much he wants me, the hard length of him straining against the dark fabric. The sight makes my core ache with renewed need.

"Touch me, Stella," he says, his voice strained.

I hook my fingers in the waistband of his briefs and pull them down, freeing him completely. He's impressive, and the knowledge that this is mine, that he's this hard for me, makes me feel powerful in a way I've never experienced before.

I wrap my hand around him tentatively, marveling at the

contrast of soft skin over steel. He groans, and his head falls back against the pillow.

"Like this?" I ask, stroking him slowly.

"Grip me tighter, like this." He wraps his hand around mine and guides me up and down his thick shaft. Precum starts to leak out of his tip, and I rub my thumb across it, smearing it as I learn the pressure and pace he likes.

"Lick it," he tells me. When I lean down to taste him, he makes a sound that goes straight to my core.

"Stella, fuck—"

I pull back. "Good?"

"So good." He brings his thumb to my mouth and pulls down my bottom lip. "Open for me, Stella."

My mouth slides over his tip, and he guides his cock into me gently, teaching me what he likes without making me feel foolish. His responses are immediate and honest, and I find myself getting lost in the power of it, in how I can make this strong, confident man fall apart with just my mouth.

"You're incredible at this," he pants. "So fucking good."

The praise makes me bold, and I take him deeper, loving how he trembles beneath me. I'm actually enjoying this, which is a revelation. One hand grips the base of him, helping me guide him in and out of my mouth, while his other hand is tangled in my hair. I can feel his arms tense, like he's trying to hold back, trying to be gentle.

"I'm close," he warns. "Lay on your back."

I pull back, and he flips me on the bed and finishes over me, across my stomach and chest, his release warm on my skin.

"Oh, fuck, Stella." He leans down to kiss me, careful not

to make more of a mess. "That was fucking incredible. Your mouth is going to be the death of me."

"Shower?" I suggest against his lips.

"Definitely."

The hot water feels incredible on my skin, but not as incredible as Brandon's hands roaming all over my body with the slick soap. When he presses me against the tile wall, I'm already ready for him again, and I can feel he's ready for me, too.

"I don't have any protection with me."

"I have an IUD," I say softly. "And I haven't been with anyone since my last test. What about you?"

"Clean bill of health, and it's been months for me." His thumb traces across my wrist.

"I want to feel all of you," I tell him.

He slides into me with a groan. "Fuck you are so tight, Stella."

The pleasure is instant. I'm ready to explode. "Don't stop. Keep going."

The angle is perfect, and he's hitting spots that make me see stars. We move together desperately, all the finesse from earlier replaced by raw need. When I come apart around him, he follows immediately, burying his face in my neck.

We dry each other off slowly, our hands lingering longer than necessary. When Brandon wraps the towel around my shoulders and pulls me against him, I can feel he's already getting hard again.

"Bed?" he murmurs against my ear.

I nod, and he lifts me up. My legs wrap around his waist as he carries me the few steps to his bedroom.

Later, wrapped in his arms with my head on his chest, it's like we've unleashed Pandora's box and I can say with confidence there is no way to put these feelings back into it. I think about how everything has changed. How I can't imagine going back to being just friends after this.

"What are you thinking about?" he murmurs, his fingers tracing patterns on my bare shoulder.

"How we're going to be exhausted tomorrow," I say instead of the truth.

He laughs, and the sound rumbles through his chest. "Worth it."

I'm drifting off when I feel him hardening against my hip again.

"Seriously?" I ask, but I'm already reaching for him.

"What can I say? You're addictive."

Tomorrow, we'll figure out what this means, what we are to each other. Tonight, I just want to get lost in him again and again until the sun comes up.

thirty-three

. . .

Stella

THE TANGERINE TALENT offices hum with the kind of controlled chaos that makes my heart race in the best way. Phones ringing, assistants power walking past with coffee and contracts, the distant sound of agents negotiating seven-figure deals. This is my world, and after joining Blair to help her start her own agency, I've managed to work my way up to an agent. I finally feel like I belong here.

I'm reviewing notes for my next meeting when my assistant, Tatum, pops his head into my office. "Ava St. James is here."

"Perfect. Send her in."

Ava sweeps into my office like she's making an entrance at a premiere, which, knowing her, is exactly the effect she's going for. At forty-seven, she's still stunning in that timeless Hollywood way, all sharp cheekbones and perfect posture. She's also stubborn as hell and convinced that her Oscar win fifteen years ago should be enough to carry her career forever.

"Stella, darling," she says, settling into the chair across

from my desk with the kind of grace they don't teach anymore. "I've been thinking about our last conversation."

"And?" I lean forward, trying to read her expression.

"You want me to do television." She says it like I've suggested she start doing dinner theater in Oklahoma.

"I want you to expand your horizons," I correct gently. "The landscape has changed, Ava. Some of the best roles for women are on streaming platforms and starring in limited series now. Look at what Meryl did with *Big Little Lies* or Nicole Kidman with *The Undoing*. These aren't your grandmother's TV movies."

Ava sighs, examining her perfectly manicured nails. "When I started in this business, there was a clear hierarchy. Movies were art. Television was—"

"A paycheck," I finish. "I know. But that was then. Now we have show runners like Shonda Rhimes and Mindy Kaling creating stories specifically for streaming, and they're winning Emmys and Golden Globes. We have A-listers lining up to be part of anthology series because they know that's where the meaty roles are."

I pull out the folder I've been preparing for weeks. "I've identified three projects that would be perfect for you. There's a limited series about political wives in the seventies that shoots for four months and would put you in contention for every award show next year. A recurring role on that new legal drama where you'd play the senior partner who mentors the young hotshot lawyer. And..." I pause for effect. "Beyoncé's team reached out about a cameo in her next music video."

"Beyoncé?" Ava's eyebrows rise.

"Think about it. One day of shooting, global exposure to

an entirely new generation, and you'd be working with one of the most influential artists of our time. It's not selling out, Ava. It's staying relevant."

She's quiet for a long moment, and I can practically see the wheels turning. Ava's smart. She knows her last three films barely made a ripple at the box office. She knows the offers have been getting smaller, the roles less interesting.

"You know," she says slowly, "when Blair first assigned you to my account, I thought she was pawning me off on the junior agent because my career was circling the drain."

My stomach drops a little, but I keep my expression neutral.

"I was wrong," she continues, and her voice is warm now, almost surprised. "You see possibilities where I only saw problems. You understand this business in a way that...well, frankly, I underestimated you completely."

"Thank you," I say, and I mean it. Coming from someone with Ava's experience, that's not just a compliment. It's validation.

"Set up meetings for all three projects," she says, standing and smoothing down her designer dress. "And Stella? Next time I doubt your judgment, remind me of this conversation."

As Ava stands to leave, her voice takes on a gentle, sympathetic tone. "I wasn't going to say anything, but I spoke with Helena Voss before coming here."

I look up at her, confused about where she's going with this.

"She mentioned you and Brandon aren't together anymore?"

My pen freezes halfway through signing a contract. The

words seem to echo in the suddenly too-quiet office. Brandon told Helena we aren't together?

"Well," I manage, my voice perfectly steady even as my stomach plummets, "we're working through some things."

Ava shakes her head with a small frown. "I have to say, I'm surprised after seeing you two together. I think there was something really genuine there. I hope you can work things out. Sometimes, the best relationships go through rough patches."

"I appreciate that," I say, somehow maintaining my composure as she heads out of the office.

The moment the door closes behind her, I set down my pen and stare at the wall as her words replay in my head. Why would Brandon tell Helena that we weren't together anymore? And did he tell her that before he fucked me or after?

Is that why he was quick to skip over a talk about anything last night? Does he not want to be together?

I sit there, staring at the closed door, with Ava's words echoing in my head like a broken record. Brandon told Helena we weren't together. After everything that happened between us.

My hands are shaking as I try to process what this means. Did I completely misread the situation? The thought makes my stomach churn.

I'm so lost in my spiral that I don't hear my office door open again.

"Knock, knock," Natalie's voice cuts through the fog. "Hope you don't mind me barging in, but I was in the neighborhood and thought I'd see if you might have any extra passes for that indie premiere this weekend. The one with—" She stops mid-sentence. "Hello? Earth to Stella?"

I blink, finally focusing on her concerned face. "What?"

"I've been talking for like thirty seconds, and you haven't heard a thing I've said." She settles into the chair across from my desk. "What's going on?"

"Nothing. Everything. I don't know." The words tumble out before I can stop them. "Maybe I'm an idiot. Maybe I completely misunderstood everything. Maybe he just wanted to sleep with me, and now that he has, he's done."

Natalie's eyebrows shoot up. "Okay, slow down. Who are we talking about here?"

"Brandon told Helena we're not together anymore," I say, my voice cracking slightly. "After we... God, maybe I'm terrible in bed. Maybe he realized he doesn't actually want me, and now he's trying to figure out how to let me down easy."

"Wait. Hold up." Natalie leans forward. "You and Brandon slept together?"

I nod miserably. "Last night. And the night before. And this morning. It was incredible, Natalie. Like everything-I-didn't-know-I-was-missing incredible. But then he goes and tells Helena Voss that we're just friends? That we're not together?"

"Tell me who Helena is."

"She's this director he's trying to work with. And she's gorgeous, by the way. And successful. And probably closer to his age than I am." I can hear my voice getting higher, more frantic. "Maybe he realized he could do better. Maybe he was just being nice because we were fake dating and things got out of hand."

"Stella—"

"I should have known better," I continue, the words pouring out like a dam has burst. "Brandon doesn't do relationships. He's told me that himself. He keeps things casual, keeps things fun. And here I am, catching feelings like some pathetic—"

"Stop." Natalie's voice cuts through my rambling. "Just stop for a second and breathe."

I take a shaky breath.

"Now, tell me exactly what happened. From the beginning."

I tell her everything. About Brandon and me. And then about Ava's casual bomb that Brandon told Helena we weren't together anymore.

"And you haven't talked to him about this?" Natalie asks when I finish.

"How can I? What am I supposed to say? 'Hey, I heard through the Hollywood grapevine that you told someone we're not dating. Was last night just a pity fuck?'"

"First of all, stop calling yourself pathetic and stop assuming the worst. You're spiraling." Natalie stands. "Second, this calls for wine. You're staying at my place tonight so we can properly analyze this situation without you torturing yourself alone."

My phone buzzes on my desk. Brandon's name flashes on the screen.

"Don't answer that yet," Natalie says, reading over my shoulder as I pick it up.

BRANDON

> Hey, want to hang out tonight? Have to get to bed early for an early call tomorrow, but we could grab dinner or just watch something?

My heart does that stupid flutter thing it always does when I see his name, even though I'm furious, hurt, and confused.

"What do I say?" I ask Natalie.

"Something neutral that buys you time to think."

STELLA

> Natalie just walked in with a girlfriend crisis and will probably be late. Catch up tomorrow?

BRANDON

> Definitely tomorrow. Have fun with the girl talk and sleep well.

I stare at the simple message, looking for hidden meaning that probably isn't there.

"Come on," Natalie says, grabbing my purse from behind my desk. "Let's go get wine and figure out what's really going on here. Because I have a feeling this is all a big misunderstanding."

I hope she's right. But right now, it feels like my heart is breaking.

thirty-four

. . .

Stella

THE WONDERLAND STUDIOS lot feels massive when you're looking for one specific soundstage among dozens. I've been here plenty of times for client meetings, but today, I'm wandering around Stage 12 with sweaty palms and a racing heart, looking for Brandon.

After a night of wine and brutal honesty with Natalie, I've come to a decision. I need answers. Not assumptions, not secondhand information filtered through the Hollywood rumor mill, but actual answers from Brandon himself about what he told Helena and why.

Natalie was annoyingly logical about the whole thing. "Maybe he didn't want to tell her something he hadn't discussed with you first," she'd said around midnight, when we were both wine-drunk and philosophical. "Maybe he was protecting your privacy."

"Or maybe he was protecting himself," I countered.

"Only one way to find out."

So, here I am, clutching a visitor's pass and trying not to

look like a fangirl. Through the open doors, I can see the interior of a film set. Crew members are moving around purposefully, cameras are being positioned at precise angles, and somewhere in the middle of it all is Brandon.

I spot him near what looks like a fight scene setup, talking with Tony Ricci and another stunt performer. He's wearing his usual on-set uniform of jeans and a black t-shirt, his hair slightly messed up like he's been running his hands through it. Even from this distance, I can see the energy radiating from him as he gestures, explaining something with the kind of passion that made me fall for him in the first place.

The thought stops me cold. Fall for him. When did I start thinking about it in those terms?

A production assistant with a clipboard notices me hovering near the entrance. "Can I help you find someone?"

"I'm here to see Brandon Grimaldi," I say, showing her my pass. "I can wait until he's finished."

She glances at the group near the fight setup. "They're just finishing up the safety briefing for the next scene. Should be another few minutes."

I nod and find a spot out of the way where I can watch without being obvious about it. The butterflies in my stomach are doing aerial acrobatics as I rehearse what I'm going to say. Nothing accusatory. Nothing dramatic. Just honest questions that deserve honest answers.

Brandon must sense that someone is watching him, because he looks up from his conversation and scans the room. When his eyes find mine, his face lights up with surprise and something that looks like genuine happiness. He holds up one finger in a "just a minute" gesture and says something to Tony before jogging over to where I'm standing.

"Hey," he says, slightly out of breath and grinning like seeing me just made his entire day better. "What are you doing here? Not that I'm complaining."

The warmth in his voice throws me off balance. This isn't the reaction of someone who's trying to distance himself from me. This is Brandon looking at me like I'm exactly who he wanted to see.

"I wanted to talk to you about something," I say, my carefully rehearsed words suddenly feeling inadequate. "When you have a minute."

"Of course. We're just about to run through this fight sequence, but it should only take about twenty minutes. Can you wait?"

Before I can answer, Tony calls out, "Brandon! We're ready for the run-through."

"Go," I say, gesturing toward the set. "I'll wait right here."

Brandon hesitates for a moment, like he wants to say something else. Then he leans down and presses a quick kiss to my forehead. "I'm really glad you're here," he murmurs against my skin.

The casual intimacy of the gesture, done without thinking in front of his colleagues, makes my heart skip. I watch as he jogs back to Tony and the stunt team, my confusion growing by the minute. Maybe Natalie was right. Maybe this really is just a misunderstanding.

The crew positions themselves around the set as Brandon and another stunt performer prepare for what looks like an elaborate fight scene. Safety mats are positioned around the area, and I can see thick cables attached to harnesses that will help control their falls. Tony calls out last-minute instructions while cameras capture different angles.

It's fascinating to watch Brandon work. The way he moves with precise control, how he communicates with the other performers, and the complete focus on his face as he ensures every detail is perfect.

"Action!" the director calls.

The fight begins. Brandon and the other performer engage in what looks like a realistic brawl, their movements choreographed but convincing. They're working their way across the set, throwing punches at each other and dodging with practiced precision.

The scene calls for Brandon to be thrown backward off a platform, where his safety cable should catch him and lower him gently to the mats below. I've seen him do similar stunts dozens of times in movies, and it always looks dangerous. But I know systems are in place to keep him safe.

Brandon launches himself backward off the platform exactly as planned, his body arcing through the air. But instead of the smooth descent I expect, there's a sharp snapping sound that echoes across the soundstage.

The cable breaks.

Brandon falls the full fifteen feet, hitting the safety mats hard and rolling in a way that looks completely wrong. The mats are there to cushion a controlled landing, not to catch someone in free fall.

My breath stops. Everything stops.

Then chaos erupts as crew members rush toward where Brandon landed. Tony shouts for medics, and someone yells to shut down all cameras. But I can't move. My feet are rooted to the floor like I'm frozen in place, watching this nightmare unfold in slow motion.

"Brandon!" His name tears out of my throat before I can stop it, raw and desperate.

I can see him now, lying too still on the mats, his left arm bent at an angle that makes my stomach lurch. There's blood on his forehead where he must have hit something on the way down.

My heart is hammering so hard against my ribs that I think it might crack them. I try to move, try to run to him, but my legs feel like they're made of concrete. The sound that came out of me when he hit the ground—was that me screaming? I can't remember making that sound, but my throat feels raw.

"Call an ambulance!" Tony shouts, kneeling beside Brandon while other crew members clear the area.

That breaks the spell. I'm running before I realize I'm moving, pushing past people, my hands shaking so violently I can barely control them. But someone catches my arm before I can reach him.

"Ma'am, please step back. Let the medics work."

I want to fight them, want to shove past and get to Brandon, but I can't catch my breath long enough to argue. I watch from a few feet away as they check his pulse, carefully examine his arm, and shine a light in his eyes. And all I can think is that I came here to ask him about some stupid miscommunication when I should have just told him that I'm falling in love with him.

thirty-five

. . .

Brandon

THE FIRST THING I'm aware of is the beeping. Steady, electronic, the kind of sound that immediately tells you you're somewhere you don't want to be. Hospital. The air smells like disinfectant and floor wax, with an underlying medicinal sharpness that makes my throat feel scratchy.

The second thing is the dull ache radiating from my left arm, which feels heavy and wrong in a way that suggests it's been immobilized. When I try to flex my fingers, something hard and rough scrapes against the thin hospital blanket. I realize I'm in a cast from my hand to just below my elbow.

The third thing is warmth. Someone's holding my right hand, and their skin is soft against my palm, anchoring me to consciousness.

My eyes blink open, and my mouth tastes like cotton and something metallic, likely from whatever painkillers they've pumped into me.

The room is dim, but not dark, with that twilight hospital

lighting that never lets you know what time it is. The bed feels too narrow, the mattress firm in that institutional way, and beneath the strong smell of astringent is something more familiar.

Then I see Stella.

She's sitting in the plastic hospital chair, pulled up close to my bed, her fingers interlaced with mine, and she looks like she's been crying. Her hair is messier than usual, and there are mascara smudges under her eyes that she hasn't bothered to wipe away. The hint of vanilla and citrus is almost healing when I catch a whiff.

"Hey," I manage, my voice dry and rough like I've been swallowing sandpaper.

"Oh, thank God." The relief in her voice is so profound that it makes my chest tight. "How do you feel?"

"Like I fell off a building." I try to sit up and immediately think better of it when my head protests with a sharp spike of pain. The room tilts slightly, and I have to close my eyes until it settles. "What happened? Last thing I remember was that cable snapping."

"Fifteen-foot fall when your safety line broke," Stella says, and her grip on my hand tightens. "You've got a broken arm and a concussion, but the doctor said you're incredibly lucky. The way you managed to adjust mid-fall and hit the mats probably saved you from much worse."

"How long was I out?"

"About three hours. They had to set your arm and do some scans to make sure there was no internal bleeding." She reaches over to brush hair off my forehead with her free hand.

"Tony said you knew exactly what to do when the cable snapped. That your experience saved you."

The touch is gentle, careful, but I can feel her hand trembling slightly. "Hey, I'm okay. Really."

"You could have died, Brandon." Her voice cracks on the words. "When I saw you fall, when you weren't moving, I thought I was going to lose you before I ever got to tell you..."

She trails off, but something in her expression makes my heart rate pick up, which apparently registers on the monitor because it starts beeping faster.

"Tell me what?" I ask softly.

Stella takes a shaky breath, and her eyes meet mine with an intensity that makes everything else fade away. "That I'm in love with you. That I have been for weeks, maybe months, and I was too scared to admit it. That what happened between us wasn't just physical for me, and I don't care if it was just that for you because I needed you to know."

The words hit me like a physical force, and for a moment, I can't breathe. "Stella—"

"I know you told Helena we weren't together," she continues, the words tumbling out like she's afraid I'll stop her. "And I know you probably have good reasons, and maybe you were just being kind by not rejecting me outright, but sitting in that waiting room, thinking you might never wake up, made me realize that I'd rather risk everything than spend another day pretending I don't love you."

"Stop," I say, squeezing her hand to get her attention. "Just stop for a second."

She looks at me with those blue eyes, which are bright

with tears, and I feel something settle into place in my chest. Something that's been trying to find its way there for months.

"You think I told Helena we weren't together because I don't want to be with you?"

"I don't know, maybe?"

"Stella." I bring our joined hands to my lips and press a soft kiss to her knuckles. "I told Helena we were just friends because we hadn't talked about what we are yet. I didn't want to tell anyone anything until you and I figured out what we wanted this to be."

"What do you want it to be?" she whispers.

"Everything," I say without hesitation. "I want everything with you. I want to wake up next to you every morning. I want to take you to family dinners and listen to you charm my sisters. I want to fight about what to watch on TV and make up by doing things that would scandalize your mother."

She laughs through her tears, and the sound warms my chest.

"I want to support your career and have you support mine. I want to be the person you call when you have good news and the person who holds you when you have bad news." I pause, my thumb tracing across her knuckles. "I want to love you, Stella. Openly, honestly, for as long as you'll let me."

"You love me?" The question is barely a whisper.

"I'm completely gone for you," I admit. "Have been since the first time you made me laugh during one of those terrible reality shows. Maybe even before that. You snuck up on me, sunshine. One day, we were friends, and the next, I couldn't imagine my life without you in it."

She leans forward, bringing her face closer to mine, and I can see the exact moment she decides to believe me. "I love you, too. So much it scares me."

"Good," I say, using my good hand to cup her cheek. "Because anything worth having should be a little scary."

When she kisses me, it's soft and sweet and tastes like tears and promises, and I pour everything I've been feeling into it: the fear when I realized I was falling, the relief of waking up to her face, and the overwhelming gratitude that she's here and she's mine.

"I'm sorry I doubted you," she murmurs against my lips. "I should have just asked instead of assuming the worst."

"I'm sorry I didn't tell you how I felt sooner. I kept thinking I had time, that I could figure out the perfect way to say it." I brush my thumb across her cheek. "Turns out there's no perfect timing for this stuff."

She smiles against my mouth. "Maybe the timing was exactly right. Sometimes, it takes almost losing something to realize how much it means to you."

"Is that your way of saying you're glad I fell off a building?"

"Don't joke about that." Her expression grows serious, and she pulls back just enough to look me in the eyes. "When I saw you fall..." She shakes her head. "I can't lose you, Brandon. Not when I just got you."

"Hey." I squeeze her hand. "I'm not going anywhere. I'm tougher than I look."

"You better be because, now that we've figured this out, I have plans for you that require you to be in one piece." Her smile returns, but there's still worry in her eyes. "Speaking of which, you need to focus on getting better. No more stunts until you're completely cleared."

"What about the F1 project? Did Helena—"

"Already handled," Stella says with a smile. "I may have made a few calls while you were unconscious. Helena knows what happened, and she's holding the position for you. She said anyone tough enough to walk away from a fifteen-foot fall is exactly who she wants coordinating her stunts."

"You called Helena?"

"I called everyone I could think of to make sure this accident didn't hurt your career. That's what partners do for each other." She pauses, and color rises in her cheeks. "If that's what we are. Partners."

"Partners," I repeat, testing the word. It fits perfectly. "I like the sound of that."

"Good, because I'm not going anywhere. You're stuck with me, Grimaldi."

"Promise?"

"Promise." She leans forward to kiss me again, and this time, there's nothing tentative about it. It's the kiss of a woman who knows exactly what she wants and isn't afraid to claim it.

When we break apart, we're both breathing harder, and I'm reminded of all the reasons I fell for her in the first place. Her strength, her loyalty, the way she makes everything in my life better just by being part of it.

"I should probably call my family," I say reluctantly. "They're going to lose their minds when they find out I'm in the hospital."

"Already done. I called Nina while you were in surgery."

Stella's cheeks flush slightly. "She had a lot of questions about who I was and why I was calling, so I just said I was your neighbor and close friend. Emergency contact. That seemed to satisfy her enough to keep her from booking the next flight to LAX."

"Oh, no." I groan, though I'm smiling. "Stella, you have no idea what you've just done. My family has been waiting for this moment for years."

"What do you mean?"

"I mean, they've given up hope that I'll ever settle down. And now, suddenly, there's someone calling about me from a hospital?" I shake my head. "I hope you're ready for the backlash."

"What do you mean?"

"Oh, they're going to want to meet you immediately."

Her eyes widen slightly. "Meet me?"

"You know, we do this big Fourth of July thing every year at my parents' place in the Hamptons. You should come with me." The words come out before I've really thought them through, but the moment I say them, I know I mean it. "I mean, if you want to. It's pretty overwhelming. My whole family descends, and it gets loud and chaotic."

"You've never brought anyone home," she says quietly, and it's not a question.

"No. Never had anyone I wanted them to meet." I pause, studying her face. "But I want them to know you. I want you to be part of that."

She's quiet for a moment, and I can see her processing what this means. Then she reaches up to touch my cheek, and her thumb traces my jawline.

"I'd love to meet your family," she says softly. "On one condition. You have to be my plus-one for the charity gala my mom already tried to invite you to."

"Deal." I catch her hand and press it against my cheek. "Now, crawl up in here with me so I can kiss you."

thirty-six

. . .

Stella

TWO DAYS LATER, Brandon is finally cleared to go home. His arm is in a proper cast now, bright blue because, apparently, he has the sense of humor of a twelve-year-old, and the concussion symptoms have mostly faded. The doctor's only instruction was to rest and take it easy.

The elevator in our building is occupied when the doors open, and Mason is standing there with a tennis racket bag slung over his shoulder, looking like he just came from the courts. My stomach does a little flip, not from attraction but from the awkwardness of running into him with Brandon right beside me.

"Stella! Brandon!" Mason's face lights up with genuine warmth. "How are you feeling, man? I heard about the accident."

"Much better, thanks," Brandon says, lifting his cast slightly. "Just have to take it easy for a while."

"That's good to hear." Mason turns to me with that easy smile I used to find so appealing. "Actually, Stella, I was going to text you again. I wanted to see if maybe you were free to meet up at the club this weekend? I'd love to get some pointers on my game. We could grab dinner after."

I feel Brandon's hand find mine, a simple gesture of support that doesn't try to control the situation. When I look at him, there's no jealousy or insecurity in his expression, just quiet confidence in us. It makes my response feel easy and honest.

"That's really sweet of you to offer," I say, turning back to Mason, "but Brandon and I are actually dating now."

"Oh!" Mason's eyebrows shoot up in surprise before his expression shifts to genuine happiness. "That's awesome. Congratulations, you two. I have to say, I'm not totally shocked. There always seemed to be something between you guys."

"We're pretty happy about it," Brandon says simply, his thumb brushing across my knuckles.

"Well, I'm really happy for you both," Mason says as the elevator reaches our floor. "Take care of that arm."

As we go our separate ways, I lean into Brandon's side, feeling lighter than I have in months.

"That went well," Brandon observes.

"It did. I was worried it might be awkward, but it felt good to say it out loud. That we're together."

"It felt good to hear it."

We settle inside his apartment and finally relax on the couch.

"Nina's been texting me nonstop," Brandon says, scrolling through his phone with his good hand. "She wants to FaceTime tonight so the whole family can meet you properly."

"Tonight?"

"Unless you're not ready for that level of chaos? I can put them off."

Meeting his entire family over video chat feels like a big step, but there's something exciting about taking this next step with him.

"Let's do it," I say. "I want to meet them."

An hour later, we're positioned on his couch with his laptop balanced on the coffee table, waiting for the call to connect. When the screen fills with faces, I'm immediately overwhelmed by the sheer energy radiating through the camera.

"Brandon!" A woman who must be his mother appears front and center, and her face lights up when she sees him. "You look terrible. Are you eating enough? Have you been sleeping?"

"I'm fine, Ma. The cast comes off in six weeks, and I feel great." He gestures toward me. "This is Stella."

The response is immediate and overwhelming: multiple voices talking at once, sisters pushing each other out of the way to get closer to the camera, his father's booming voice cutting through the chaos to welcome me to the family.

"She's gorgeous!" one sister declares.

"I can't believe you finally brought someone home!" another adds.

"Virtually home," Brandon corrects with a laugh.

"Close enough," his mother says firmly. "Stella, dear, it's so wonderful to meet you. Thank you for taking care of our boy. When Nina told us there was a woman calling from the hospital, we didn't know what to think."

"She's been amazing," Brandon says as his thumb traces circles on my hand. "I couldn't have asked for better care."

"We hear you're coming for Fourth of July," his father chimes in.

"I'm really looking forward to it," I say, and I mean it. Despite the chaos and the overlapping conversations, there's something warm and welcoming about his family that makes me feel instantly included.

The call goes on for another twenty minutes, and by the time we hang up, my cheeks hurt from smiling.

"They're wonderful," I say, settling against his good side.

"They love you already. I can tell." His fingers trace gentle patterns along my arm.

He turns his head to look at me, his expression soft. "You've made me happier than I knew was possible."

The sincerity in his voice makes my heart flutter. I shift slightly, angling my body toward his, and something changes in the air between us. The playful comfort transforms into something warmer, more charged.

"Brandon?" I murmur as my hand finds the hem of his shirt.

"Yeah?"

"I know the doctor said you need to rest, but I was thinking maybe I could do most of the work this time."

His breath catches as understanding dawns. "Stella."

"I want to take care of you," I say, already moving to straddle his hips with careful precision. "Let me take care of you."

"You don't have to convince me," he says, his good hand sliding up my thigh. "Tell me what to do, sunshine."

I silence him with a kiss, pouring all my love and need into it. When we break apart, we're both breathing hard.

"I've been thinking about this all day," I whisper against his lips. "About how I almost lost you before I could tell you how much you mean to me."

His thumb traces my bottom lip. "You're not going to lose me. Ever."

"Promise?" I breathe, and something in his expression shifts, becomes vulnerable and hungry all at once.

"Promise."

Getting undressed turns out to be a slow-motion process that borders on exquisite torture. I start with his shirt, my fingers careful and deliberate as I work the fabric over his cast and good arm.

"Sorry," I whisper when he winces slightly.

"Don't be sorry," he says, his voice rough. "Don't stop."

I move closer, my hands exploring the expanse of his chest, careful around the fading bruises. The urge to kiss every mark, every place he was hurt, overwhelms me. "I hate that you were hurt."

"I'm okay," he says, catching my hand and bringing it to his lips. "I'm more than okay."

"Bedroom," I murmur against his mouth.

He nods, and I help him stand before leading him slowly down the hallway. Once we reach his room, I guide him to sit on the edge of the bed, my hands already tracing the edge of his waistband.

As I trail kisses down his chest, my hands map every inch

of skin I can reach. When I reach his jeans, I kneel between his legs, looking up at him as I work open the button. The sight of me on my knees in front of him makes his breath catch.

"Stella," he warns, but his voice is strained with want.

I carefully work the denim down his legs, and my knuckles brush against him through his boxers in ways that make him tense. When I look up at him, his pupils are blown wide with desire.

"Let me take care of you," I whisper as my hands skim up his thighs.

When I free him from his boxers and take him in my mouth, he groans my name like a prayer. He's hot and hard against my tongue, and the way he responds to every movement I make sends heat pooling low in my belly. I work him slowly, savoring the weight of him, the way his good hand tangles in my hair, the soft sounds he makes when I swirl my tongue just right.

"Fuck, that feels so good," he gasps, his hips lifting slightly. "But if you keep doing that, I'm going to come, and I need to be inside you first."

"Lay back," I say, pressing kisses along his hipbone.

"Wait." His good hand reaches for me, helping me stand. "Undress, Stella," he commands, his fingers finding the hem of my shirt. "I want to see all of you first."

I help him remove my clothes, and his eyes drink in every inch of skin as it's revealed. When I'm finally naked before him, he goes completely still.

"God, you're beautiful," he breathes, and his hand skims up my ribs to cup my breast. "I can't believe you're mine."

"I'm yours," I whisper, leaning into his touch. "All yours."

I crawl over him, pushing him back gently onto the bed, and when I sink onto him, we both go perfectly still. The sensation of him inside me feels intimate in a way that fills me with emotion. He fills me completely, and the feeling of connection is so intense that it brings tears to my eyes.

"God, Stella," he breathes, his good hand gripping my hip. "You feel incredible."

I start to move slowly, carefully, taking control so he doesn't have to worry about his arm. The angle is perfect, hitting spots that make me gasp and arch against him. The way he's looking at me like I'm something precious and powerful makes me feel beautiful.

"You're perfect," he whispers, his eyes never leaving my face. "So fucking perfect."

His good hand slides up my body to cup my breast, and his thumb brushes my nipple in a way that makes me moan. I lean down to kiss him, swallowing his groans as I move against him, our bodies finding a rhythm that's uniquely ours.

His fingers work expertly, circling and pressing while I move above him. The dual sensation of him inside me and his touch where I'm most sensitive builds the tension to an almost unbearable level.

"Brandon," I whimper, and my head falls back as the pleasure builds.

"That's it," he encourages, his voice rough with his own need. "Let go for me."

The combination of his touch and his words sends me over the edge, and my body clenches around him as pleasure crashes through me in waves that seem to go on forever. The sight and feel of me coming undone triggers his own release, and he follows moments later with a groan that sounds like my name.

Afterwards, we lie tangled together, both of us breathing hard. I'm sprawled across his chest, careful to keep my weight off his injured arm, and I can feel his heartbeat slowly returning to normal beneath my cheek.

"I love you," I say against his skin.

"I love you, too," he replies, his fingers trailing through my hair.

And as he pulls me up for another kiss, I know with absolute certainty that this is exactly where I'm meant to be.

thirty-seven

. . .

Stella

"STOP FIDGETING WITH YOUR BOW TIE," I say, watching Brandon adjust it for the fourth time in the bathroom mirror. "You look perfect."

"Easy for you to say. You're not about to meet your girl-friend's father for the first time." He runs his good hand through his hair, careful not to mess up the styling. His cast comes off next week, and he's been counting down the days.

I step behind him, smooth down his collar, and meet his eyes in the mirror. "My father is going to love you. Just like everyone else does."

"I hope your mother put in a good word for me. She loves me," he says as he gives me a wink. He knows good and well how much my mother adores him.

"I'm sure she did." I tease him.

His phone buzzes on the counter, and he glances down at it. His entire expression changes, with tension melting into relief and excitement.

"Helena?" I ask.

He nods and turns the phone so I can see the message.

HELENA

Welcome to the PACE team, Brandon. Just emailed the shoot schedule for the next six weeks.

Looking forward to working with you.

This is going to be incredible.

"Brandon, that's amazing!" I throw my arms around him, careful of his cast. "I'm so proud of you."

"Coordinating instead of performing," he says, still staring at the message like he can't quite believe it. "This is really happening."

"This is just the beginning," I tell him, meaning every word. "You're going to be brilliant at this. Better than you ever were at throwing yourself off buildings."

"Think so?"

"I know so." I reach up to fix his bow tie one last time. "Now, come on. Let's go show my parents what a power couple looks like."

Crystal chandeliers cast warm light across the marble floors, where designer gowns and tailored tuxedos mingle beneath soaring ceilings draped in ivory silk. The air hums with champagne glasses clinking and the gentle murmur of guests discussing their latest philanthropic endeavors over the scent of white orchids arranged in towering centerpieces. It's exactly the kind of elegant venue that makes my father's company events feel important.

We make our way through the crowd, and I can feel Brandon's nervous energy beside me.

"There's my beautiful daughter," my father's voice booms as he approaches with open arms. "You look radiant, sweetheart."

"Thanks, Daddy." I hug him tightly, then turn to Brandon. "This is Brandon Grimaldi. Brandon, my father, Robert Rhodes."

"Mr. Rhodes, it's an honor to meet you," Brandon says, extending his hand.

"The honor's mine," my father replies, giving Brandon the kind of firm handshake that's meant to take the measure of a man. "I've heard wonderful things about you."

"Thank you, sir."

"Stella tells me you coordinate stunt scenes for films?"

"I do. Actually, I just got confirmation today that I'll be working on a new racing series for the next six weeks. It's a big change for me career-wise."

"Congratulations. That sounds like exciting work." My father's approval is evident in his voice.

"Your daughter convinced me it was time to use my brain instead of just my body," Brandon says with a smile.

"Smart woman, my Stella. Always has been."

The conversation flows easily from there, and I can see my father genuinely warming to Brandon. They talk about work, about Los Angeles, about Brandon's family in New York.

"There you are," my mother says as she approaches. "You look stunning, Stella. And Brandon, you look very handsome tonight."

"Thank you, Mrs. Rhodes. You look beautiful."

"Such a charmer." She beams at him, then turns to me.

"Darling, I was just talking to Patricia Wrigley about her daughter's wedding. Such a lovely affair. Of course, she had the advantage of planning for two years."

"Mama," I warn.

"I was just wondering if you've given marriage any more thought."

"We haven't been together that long." I grip Brandon's hand tightly. I'm not embarrassed about her asking me about marrying Brandon. Honestly, I think he would probably marry me today if I wanted him to. It's that my mother needs to know that I don't *have* to marry him.

"I know, sweetheart, but when you know, you know. And Brandon seems like such a stable, reliable man. The kind who could really take care of you."

"Actually, Mrs. Rhodes," Brandon says gently, "I think it's more that we take care of each other. Stella's incredibly capable on her own."

"Of course she is, but surely, there's room for other priorities as well. Family, stability, and she can step back from work when the time comes."

Something inside me snaps. Heat floods my chest and spreads up my neck like a wildfire. My hands are trembling slightly, but not from nerves; no, instead, it's from years of swallowed words finally demanding to be spoken. This is it, the moment I've been avoiding my entire life, and my heart is hammering so hard I can hear it in my ears.

"Mama, stop." The words come out sharper than I intended, but I don't take them back. My voice sounds stronger and more certain than I've ever heard it. "My career isn't a temporary thing until something better comes along.

This is my life. This is what I've chosen, and I'm not going to apologize for it."

Brandon steps closer to me and wraps his arm around my waist in a show of support. The warmth of his hand on my hip steadies me, gives me the courage to keep going even as my mother's eyes widen in shock.

"Sweetheart, I just think—"

"No." I shake my head. Adrenaline makes my skin feel electric, and every nerve in my body is singing with the rush of finally speaking my truth. "I love you, but I'm not going to make myself smaller to fit into someone else's idea of what my life should look like. I'm successful, I'm happy, and Brandon supports that completely."

The words taste like freedom on my tongue, even as my stomach churns with the fear of having disappointed her. But underneath that fear is relief so profound it makes my knees weak.

My mother's face cycles through several emotions: surprise, hurt, and finally something that might be under-standing.

"You're absolutely right," my father says quietly, stepping closer to us. "Your mother and I are proud of you, Stella. Everything you've accomplished."

"We are proud," my mother says after a moment, her voice softer now. "I just want you to be happy."

"I am happy, Mama. Really, truly happy."

She looks between Brandon and me, and I can see her processing what just happened. "You really meant what you said, didn't you? About supporting her career?"

"Completely," Brandon says without hesitation. "I fell in

love with Stella exactly as she is. I love that she's ambitious, driven, and passionate about her work. I'd never want to change that."

"Even if it means late nights and travel and putting work first sometimes?"

"Especially then. Caroline, your daughter is extraordinary at what she does. The world needs more women like her in positions of power, not fewer."

My mother is quiet for a long moment, and I can see her adjusting her expectations in real time. Finally, she reaches over and squeezes Brandon's arm.

"I can see why she chose you," she says softly. "You really do see her, don't you?"

"Every day," he replies as his eyes find mine.

My mother nods, and something settles in her expression. "Well then. I suppose I need to adjust my dreams of garden parties and Junior League meetings."

"You could always dream about film premieres and award shows instead," I suggest tentatively.

She laughs, and for the first time tonight, it sounds completely genuine. "You know what? I think I could get used to that."

The tension breaks, and conversation resumes around us. My father claps Brandon on the shoulder with obvious approval, and my mother wraps me in a hug, her way of apologizing and approving of me.

"Want to get some air?" Brandon murmurs in my ear a few minutes later.

I nod, and he leads me to the hotel's terrace. The night air is warm, and the city lights twinkle below us.

"I'm proud of you," he says as soon as we're alone. "That took real courage."

"It felt good. Scary, but good." I lean against the railing, processing what just happened. "I can't believe I actually stood up to her."

"I can. You're the strongest person I know."

He moves to stand behind me and wraps his good arm around my waist. We stand like that for a moment, looking out over the city, both of us processing the evening.

"Stella," he says finally, his voice serious. "I have something to ask you."

I turn in his arms, studying his face. "What is it?"

He reaches into his jacket pocket and pulls out a key. "There's a two-bedroom opening up in our building. Better kitchen, bigger living space, amazing view of the city."

My heart starts racing as I realize what he's asking.

"Move in with me," he says, his eyes intense. "Not across the hall, not as neighbors who sometimes sleep over. Really move in. Build something together."

"Brandon."

"I know it's a big step." He pauses, choosing his words carefully. "I don't want to waste any more time. I want to wake up with you every morning and fall asleep with you every night. I want to merge our lives completely."

I look at this man who sees exactly who I am and loves me for it, who supports my dreams instead of asking me to shrink them, who just watched me have the hardest conversation of my life and couldn't be prouder.

"Yes," I breathe. "Yes, absolutely yes."

epilogue

. . .

Brandon

THE GRIMALDI FAMILY Fourth of July party in the Hamptons is in full swing, and I'm watching Stella charm my entire extended family like she was born to it. She's sitting on the deck with my grandmother, listening intently to stories about the old neighborhood in Brooklyn, while my youngest nephew shows her his collection of seashells.

Nina appears at my elbow with two beers. "She's perfect for you. I haven't seen you this happy since...well, ever."

"She is pretty amazing," I agree, accepting the drink gratefully. The ring box in my pocket feels like it weighs ten pounds, and I've been fighting nerves all afternoon.

"You nervous about tonight?"

"Terrified," I admit. "What if she says no?"

Nina gives me a look that suggests I might be the dumbest person alive. "Brandon, that woman looks at you like you hung the moon. She's not going to say no."

"Easy for you to say. You're not about to propose to the most incredible woman on the planet."

"Trust me, any woman who moves across the country to go to college and then stays to build her own career isn't going to walk away from love when she finds it."

Nina gives me one more encouraging smile before heading back to the party. A few minutes later, Stella approaches with her phone in hand, looking puzzled.

"Everything okay?" I ask.

"Just Natalie. She's heading to Jake's Fourth of July party." She pauses, looking confused. "Which is weird because I didn't know they were that close. Since when does Natalie hang out with Jake?"

I file that information away as interesting but not immediately relevant. "Maybe they bonded over being the only single people in our friend group?"

"Maybe," she says, but she still looks confused.

The sun is starting to set, painting the sky in brilliant oranges and pinks. Perfect timing.

"Want to take a walk on the beach?" I suggest casually. "The fireworks should start soon, and the view is better down there."

"That sounds perfect."

We make our way down the wooden stairs to the private beach, hand in hand. The sand is cool under our feet, and the lapping of the waves provides the perfect backdrop. In the distance, I can hear my family's laughter drifting from the deck above.

"This has been incredible," Stella says, stopping to face the water. "Your family is wonderful. I can see where you get your charm."

"They love you. My mother hasn't stopped talking about how smart and beautiful you are."

"She's been showing me photos of you as a baby. You were adorable."

"Were?"

She laughs and bumps my shoulder with hers. "Still are."

The first firework explodes overhead, casting colorful light across the water. It's time.

"Stella," I say, my heart hammering against my ribs.

"Mmm?" She's still watching the sky, mesmerized by the display.

I drop to one knee in the sand behind her.

"Turn around."

She does, and her hands immediately fly to her mouth when she sees me kneeling there with the ring box open.

"Brandon," she breathes.

"Before you panic, I know I only asked you to move in with me like a week ago. And this isn't me asking you to be my wife so I can take care of you. This is me asking you to be my partner so we can take care of each other."

Tears are already streaming down her face, but she's smiling.

"I want to spend my life with someone who challenges me and builds empires and never, ever makes herself smaller for anyone." My voice grows softer as another firework lights up her face. "I want to marry you, Stella. Not because you need me, but because I can't imagine my life without you in it."

"Me either," she whispers, then louder, "I'm getting married!"

I slip the ring onto her finger with shaking hands, then stand to pull her into a kiss. Around us, fireworks continue to explode in brilliant colors, but all I can see is her.

"I love you," she says against my lips.

"I love you, too. More than I ever thought possible."

"My mother's going to kill you, you know."

"Why?"

"You couldn't do this last week when we were in Atlanta?"

"I think she'll appreciate the setting of this proposal better. The beach, fireworks. It's pretty awesome."

"Be sure to let her know that when you tell her," she teases as she leans in for another kiss.

We stand there, holding each other on the beach, as the sky lights up above us, and I realize this is what happiness looks like. Not the performance of it, not the careful construction of it, but the real thing that happens when you find the person who sees exactly who you are and chooses you anyway.

"So," I say, grinning down at her, "ready to be a Grimaldi?"

"I've been ready since the day you helped me lie to my mother," she says, laughing through her tears.

"Best lie I ever told."

"Best truth I ever lived."

And as we head back up the beach toward my family, her hand secure in mine and her ring catching the last light of the fireworks, I know that every moment of pretending led me exactly where I was meant to be. Right here, with her, for real. She's the only truth I'll ever need.

Not ready to say goodbye to Stella and Brandon?
Scan the QR code to join my newsletter family and unlock
an exclusive bonus scene that wasn't in the book! You'll also
be the first to hear about upcoming releases, behind-the-
scenes peeks, and special offers. No spam, just bookish joy
delivered straight to your inbox!

The Backlot Series
Second Act – Available Now!
Center Stage – Available Now!
On the Record - Available Now!
Behind the Scenes - Available Now!
Off Script (Natalie and Jake) - Early 2026

Thank you!
I hope you fell in love with Stella and Brandon's journey in
Behind the Scenes! If their story captured your heart, I'd be so

grateful if you'd consider leaving a review. Reviews are like literary fairy dust for indie authors—they help other readers discover our books and help open doors we sometimes can't open ourselves without social proof. Thank you for being part of this adventure! 🤍

Before there was Stella and Brandon...
there was Blair and Wyatt.
Keep reading for the first two chapters of
Second Act
Book 1 in The Backlot Series

Available Now!
Read for free in Kindle Unlimited
https://amzn.to/41EHXFP

second act - chapter one

Blair

"Who's the hottie?"

My assistant Stella leans over my shoulder to get a closer look at my searched images of Sophia Ford, the twenty-four-year-old best actress Oscar winner, and her brother. Sophia is on my list of dream clients to represent. With any luck, I'll convince her to sign with me before summer's over. However, her brother should have received an Oscar for his role as the popular guy in high school who can make you believe anything he wants.

"His name is Wyatt Bradford, and he's not that hot."

He is that hot.

Dark blond hair, short on the sides and a little longer on the top, but in this pic, it's slicked back. His eyes gaze into the camera and are the same ice blue I remember. Still tall and still working out, I see. That shirt is struggling to stay buttoned across his toned chest. His tan suit wraps around his body, hugging his muscular thighs, and is that a crease right there, or is that...

"Ohmygod, Blair, you can see the outline of his penis!" Stella shrieks behind me.

I slam the laptop closed, stand, and walk away from the desk to get a breath of clean, Wyatt-free air and shake his memory out of my head. I haven't spoken to Wyatt in twelve years. He looks good. Exactly like a selfish dick who would lead you on and then stomp all over your heart. But still undeniably hot.

"Were you able to get passes for the *Pink Slip* season two premiere?" I ask Stella as I grab my phone. She follows me out of my office as we head down to the conference room for our team huddle.

I discovered that Sophia is obsessed with the dark comedy about managers killing off employees who aren't meeting their potential in the office. I've seen a few episodes. It reminds me of a *Hunger Games* meets *The Office* mashup. It's dark but funny.

"Of course I did." She gives me a disappointed look for daring to doubt her. "I'll have a courier bring them to her tomorrow. You still want to go, too, right? And will you have a plus-one?"

I see the look of hope in Stella's eyes, always rooting for me and my "one day it will happen" plus-one. I both love and hate that she's a hopeless romantic.

"Just me."

"Well, I've got something better than a plus-one for you. Sophia agreed to meet with you. She's shooting at Everest Studios this week and can meet between her scenes."

"The greatest thing I've ever done in my life was hire you," I say while going in for a hug.

Stella started interning for me during her senior year of college, and I hired her as soon as she graduated. It's been three years now, and we've been inseparable ever since. She's my secret weapon, and some days, I think she knows me better than I know myself.

"Oh, stop it, Blair. I hate it when you get dramatic about things that are literally in my job description." She blushes, but I know she loves the praise.

As one of the top female talent agents in this city, I have a reputation as a girl's girl. I was in law school during the #metoo movement and had a front-row seat to the shift for women. The opportunities I had to impact and support legislature during law school were historical. Too bad I only realized I didn't want to be a lawyer after I graduated.

So, I moved to LA, and in a moment of right place, right time, I met Lance Wynn. He's the CEO of The Wynn Agency—a talent agency known around Hollywood as TWA. He seduced me with the idea that I could make a difference. As an agent, I could find and sell stories that might change the world, stories that might shed light on topics like poverty, discrimination, or injustice. Plus, my background and law degree would give me a leg up in the negotiation and contract process. Lance sold me when he grabbed my hands across the bistro table we were sitting at for lunch and told me he believed women were the future of this industry.

That was my first lesson about how this town works. Tell your client whatever they want to hear to close the deal. I do focus on women—I almost exclusively sign female talent—but getting Lance to take any of my projects seriously, or prioritize them, is getting harder. After the pandemic, it's like the Hollywood mindset has reverted to "the good old days," and the scramble to make money has the industry leaning on the tried-and-true superheroes and sequels.

But I'm determined to prove the future is female. That's the reason for the Sophia Google search. Her current agent is an icon in the industry, and she's old school. Rumor has it she's retiring this fall and Sophia's looking for someone who can capitalize on her recent accolades and prevent her from being cast in stereotypical roles.

I want to represent her. I know I would be a perfect fit for her.

If Sophia agreed to meet, then it's my opportunity to lose. She wouldn't entertain the conversation if she weren't open to the idea of representation. I have some leads on a few significant projects I know she will be interested in, and I know I can convince her I'm the right choice. The premiere this week will help spotlight some of my contacts and rela-tionships, too.

"Fine. But you know it's true." I take a seat at the large conference room table while Stella joins the other assistants in the chairs along the wall. The assistants are the lifeblood of this agency, but God forbid they get a seat at the table.

When I open my laptop, the image of Wyatt is still on the screen. The search took me right down the rabbit hole to Wyatt's bio. He works for his father's law firm, which isn't a surprise, but he had other dreams.

As general counsel, Wyatt guides the firm's attorneys on a wide range of matters, including client intake, legal ethics and professional responsibility, engagement management, and policy development and compliance.

Wyatt earned his Juris Doctor from the UCLA School of Law, where he served as an editor of the UCLA Law Review. He graduated magna cum laude from the University of California, Los Angeles, with a bachelor's degree in political science and a minor in accounting.

My investigative skills must be lacking because I could only find his bio on the law firm's website. It doesn't tell me anything about if he's single or dating or what he's been doing for the last twelve years. Would it kill him to get an Instagram account? I'd even settle for a Linked In account.

"Ok, please tell me we've booked Timmy to host the *SNL* season finale," Lance says, diving right in as he pushes through the door and sits at the head of the table.

"Done. And we've booked Olivia as the musical guest, too," says Brian, another agent and Lance's pet.

Lance looks up from his phone as a grin stretches across his face. "That's what I'm talking about. Teamwork makes the dream work."

It takes all my physical control not to roll my eyes.

"When does shooting begin on *Speed 3*?" I ask. "I may need Sandy for an appearance."

"In two weeks. Just let me know, and I'll see if we can make it work." Brian leans back in his chair, feeling cocky and comfortable. Another sequel for the win.

"Blair, what about Michelle? Were you able to lock her into the lead for *Aquaman 3*?" Lance directs his question to me, but his attention is on the phone in his hand.

"Almost done. There's also a lead opportunity for her in Elizabeth's next untitled project." Yep. That gets his eyes up.

"Instead of focusing on projects that aren't a priority, perhaps you could focus on signing talent?" Lance stands and walks out before I can respond, and I take a sip of my coffee to regulate the rage bubbling under the surface.

"Ignore him," Stella says.

"Easier said than done." I grab my phone and coffee, and rise from my seat.

Stella is infringing on my personal space before I reach the exit of the conference room. "So, you gonna tell me the backstory on Wyatt?" She wiggles her eyebrows up and down, smiling at me.

I pick up my pace back to my office, trying to avoid this conversation. "I'd rather not," I mumble. Why does it feel like I can't breathe?

I'm quiet for a beat too long.

"Oh, my God—is he an ex? Did you sleep with him?" Her hands fly up to her cheeks.

I told you she knows me.

"It's ancient history."

"When? I know everyone you've dated." She puts her first and middle fingers of both hands up to air quote "dated."

"It's nothing. We went to high school together. I haven't seen him since." I play it off like it's no big deal, but my heart feels like it's being squeezed between Wyatt's metaphorical hands to remind me I'm still not over the hurt.

I've dated casually, been married—and divorced—and had no trouble recovering and moving on with my life. But one mention of Wyatt Bradford has unlocked the secret compartment of emotions I buried a long time ago.

"Do you know Sophia, too?" Stella asks.

"I don't. Well, not really. I knew Wyatt had a little sister, but she was a lot younger than us. She dropped part of her last name, so I didn't put it together immediately." I think back to one of the few times I met Sophia. Her father signed her up for a junior golf camp at the country club where I worked. She joined her father and Wyatt for lunch that week, and I was their server. I doubt she would even recall the interaction.

"He probably doesn't even remember me." I sift through the files on my desk to signal the end of this conversation. Thankfully, Stella catches on quick and just smiles before she turns to go back to her desk.

"Actually, Stella? Cancel the courier and set the meeting with Sophia for tomorrow if you can. I'll hand deliver the *Pink Slip* passes. It'll be a great icebreaker to start the conversation."

There's no reason the topic of her brother should even come up, so we can keep it buried where it belongs until I've proven I'm the right agent for her.

second act - chapter two
Wyatt

"Son! Come in here for a second."

I almost made it past him. My father is in the large conference room overlooking downtown LA, sitting in a white leather club chair surrounded by lights and cameras for his weekly *LawTalk* video web series. When in Hollywood, I suppose.

"Hey. What's the topic today?" I ask, feigning interest as I cross the room to see what he wants.

"Just a little update on California's new employment laws. You sure you don't want to join me for this?" It's the last thing on earth I want to do, especially with him.

"Can't today. Meeting Soph for lunch," I say. "Did you need something else?"

"Send her my love." He seems relieved at my rejection as he settles back into his hosting pose. "We have a new client coming in on Thursday, and I'll need you there. I'll send the details over." With a wave, I'm dismissed. He doesn't wait for questions because he doesn't allow them. Jackson Bradford has spoken, and now the conversation is over.

My grandfather started Bradford and Associates, but my father has turned it into one of the most elite law firms in the U.S. We employ over three hundred lawyers and have offices in six locations. We support a variety of sectors, but we primarily focus on mergers and acquisitions, corporate reorganizations, and shareholder activism.

Even though it's clear my future is to continue the success he's created and eventually lead the company, my father still expects me to earn partner. Too bad it's the last thing I want.

I make it down the stairs and out the door with no other interruptions and jump in the Town Car waiting for me. I haven't seen Sophia in a few weeks. She's been busy enjoying the perks of being an Oscar winner while also filming a guest-star spot on a new series for one of the streamers.

I'm so proud of her. She started acting in school plays as soon as she was able and pushed my parents to let her audition for a kids' network open call. When she landed the lead role for a new series at age twelve, it shocked all of us, but at the same time it didn't surprise us either. She was born to be in front of a camera.

There's no traffic as we wind down the side streets to Everest Studios, and I relax, knowing we'll make it there on time. She wanted to meet today because she's looking for a new agent and needs my advice. Dad and I work with a lot of the talent agencies in town, and I have some insight into the pros and cons of each one. I don't know many talent agents directly, though.

Except one.

Blair Barton. Actually, it's Bennett now. I can't believe she married someone. I used to believe that we would get married. Funny how things change. And how incredibly wrong I was.

The phone vibrates in my hand, bringing me back to the present.

SOPHIA

Almost here?

ME

Yep. What's craft services serving today?

SOPHIA

Something delicious I'm sure.

Sophia may be tiny, but she eats like a man trying to put on game-day weight. I have no idea where she puts it all.

ME

Everest catering never disappoints.

ME

Be there in 20. Love you.

SOPHIA

My phone buzzes again, and I'm expecting to see Sophia's name, but it's an email from my best friend, Jake. It's the itinerary for our annual Manmorial Weekend in San Diego—a weekend with a shit-ton of golf, whiskey, and debauchery. I look forward to it every year, but it looks like this year, Jake will be a little tame because he's engaged. He's been planning his wedding since we were in college, way before he ever had a hint of a fiancé. Jake just loves love. I shoot off a text to fuck with him a little.

ME

Is your mom joining us in La Jolla?

JAKE

What? Why would my mom be going?

ME

Oh, so she just created our itinerary then?

JAKE

Fuck you. You know I can't go to some places we typically go to.

ME

Right. You're in love. Or whatever...

I flinch, hoping I haven't reopened old wounds. I can't stand his fiancée, and Jake knows exactly how I feel. While he understands she's not for everyone, he's completely in love with her. I care deeply for Jake, and because he loves her, I do what any best friend would do—I support him the best I can.

JAKE

You should try it. Maybe someone would finally sleep with you.

ME

Hilarious.

JAKE

Where are you? Wanna grab lunch at Joan's?

ME

On my way to have lunch with Soph—
raincheck?

JAKE

Tell Soph hi...

Jake was my roommate throughout undergrad and law school. He's one of the top entertainment lawyers in LA and close to making partner at Hays and Cole, one of the best entertainment law firms in town. It's where I'd love to work and where I will never get to work. Bradford and Associates is my legacy. The minute I was born, my destiny was preordained.

As much shit as I give Jake, I get it. It must be an incredible feeling to fall in love and build a life with someone. I just don't think it's in the cards for me. I've tried. I even lived with a girl during the pandemic. However, I hate flings and one-night stands even more. Luckily, I have a few arrangements in place when the need arises.

Speak of the devil.

BETHANY

Hey love, I'm in town this week if you have
time for dinner.

ME

Can I let you know? New client starting.

BETHANY

Of course. If it can't work, I'll be back in a
few weeks.

I run my hand through my hair and catch my reflection in the rearview mirror.

What am I doing?

I should lock in time with Bethany right now. A new client won't keep me that busy. But I'm not feeling it lately. I'm in a funk. Maybe it's because Jake is getting married and I'm losing my wingman. Not that he's been a wingman for a while now.

Or maybe it's because I already had my chance at love twelve years ago. When I watched it fail spectacularly, I knew nothing else would even compare to what we had.

Read *Second Act* for free in Kindle Unlimited. Available now in Paperback and ebook from Amazon and your other favorite online bookstores.

acknowledgments

CALL SHEET

Production Title: *Behind the Scenes - The Backlot Series - Book 4*

Date: Release Day (finally!)

Location: Wherever you're reading, hopefully with snacks!

DIRECTOR

Kimberly Page, who still can't believe she gets to call this "work."

EXECUTIVE PRODUCERS

La Familia Group Text (Mom and Sisters version) – For believing in me louder than I sometimes believe in myself and the nonstop cheerleading. Oh, and texts that really are endless subplot inspiration!

Brooklynn (Gen Z Consultant & Resident Teen) – For keeping me semi-relevant online and reminding me to close my laptop once in a while.

The Besties (Cami and Holly)- I can't believe you two are still listening to me ramble on about these characters. Thank you for not being sick of me yet!

DEVELOPMENT TEAM

Nicole — The heartbeat behind the story. Thank you for your insight, your steady guidance, and the care you pour into helping me bring these characters fully to life.

Staci — The reason this book caught a reader's eye. Your design talent ensures my work looks every bit as professional as it feels personal, and I'm endlessly grateful.

Jefferson — The quiet hand behind every clean sentence. Thank you for your precision, your patience, and for saving me (and my commas) time after time.

CAST & CREW CAMEOS

Stella Rhodes – Thank you for teaching us all that faking confidence counts, and sometimes that's the bravest move of all.

Brandon Grimaldi – Insisted on his own credit. Performed all his own stunts.

SUPPORTING CAST (Real Life Edition)

Fellow Authors — Whether we've meet at The Plot Twist Book Bar, local DFW/OK bookish events, or on social media, I'm so grateful to be walking this road alongside you. Your encouragement, advice, and camaraderie have made the writing life feel less like a solo act and more like a cast I'm lucky to be part of.

Book Community Friends — Along the way, I've been lucky enough to work with so many supportive book experts - artists, branding experts, beta readers, PAs, to name a few. I'm new to so much of this and all of you I've leaned on. Thank you for the insight, creativity, and guidance that's shaped these stories (and me) for the better.

Readers — To every single one of you: thank you for picking up these books, for reading, for caring about these characters as much as I do. And to the ones who go further—who post, share, recommend, and spread the word—your enthusiasm is the reason these stories keep finding new homes. You make the dream bigger than I ever imagined!

SPECIAL THANKS

To the indie bookstores who've welcomed me with each new release—every launch brings new shop friends, and you continue to be some of the kindest, most supportive people I've ever met. I'm endlessly grateful for the space you give my stories and the heart you pour into your communities.

WRAP NOTES

This production was filmed under real-life conditions: chaotic school pickup lines, late-night edits, and way too much caffeine. Add in the weekly agony of waiting for each new episode of *The Summer I Turned Pretty*, juggling my "day job" in comms, and the pure joy of attending my very first romance book con (authors + readers = chef's kiss). All of it fed into this book in ways big and small.

And just so we're clear...if you're reading this, you're part of my crew. Thank you for helping me bring love stories to life.

about the author

Kimberly Page is a contemporary romance author who loves writing about strong heroines and the irresistible heroes who fall for them. After a career spent crafting stories for major players in the entertainment industry, she decided to create stories of her own.

When she's not writing, you can find Kimberly planning for beach time, at a theme park with her daughter, or getting lost in a good sports romance book. Follow her on TikTok and Instagram for news and updates.

www.authorkimberlypage.com